THE
EMBALMER

BY
BRAE WYCKOFF

The Embalmer
©2021. Brae Wyckoff
Published by LR Publishing

ISBN-13: 978-0-9997890-6-3
LCCN: 2021912639

Cover art by Sharon Marta
www.SharonMarta.com

Edited by Tiffany Vakilian
tiffany@tiffanyvakilian.com

ENDORSEMENTS

The Angel Killer is the scariest type of serial killer... one who thinks he's doing God's good works. *Twisted and nerve-wracking*, The Embalmer will have you double-checking the locks for weeks afterward.

Tracy Allen - Co-owner of PopHorror.com

A wild trip with teary, dramatic moments, comedic relationship moments, scary moments, and inspirational moments. *A buddy/ horror/inspirational film as a read it.* It took me places that I did not expect it would and enjoyed it immensely.

Michael Gregory- Actor in Robocop, Total Recall, Eraser, and over 400 other films in Hollywood
https://www.imdb.com/name/nm0195702/

Wow! Just finished reading The Embalmer in one sitting! I was totally engrossed! After decades in the film business, *this book NEEDS to be a movie!* I felt the character's loss, his anger, his resolve. This book carries a powerful message everyone needs to hear. I needed to hear it.

Jon Epstein
Hollywood set lighting technician for 20 years
MEN IN BLACK II - THE REVENANT - AMERICAN DREAMS - THE CLOSER

Brae Wyckoff's *The Embalmer* is an interesting mélange of *a brutal serial killer mystery, a zealous hunt, a tale of transformation*, with a born-again Alice Cooper thrown in to round out the story. The novel is populated with colorful, engaging characters and interesting locales. While some may be turned off by the language and graphic depiction of savage violence, the story should resonate with those who like their fiction dark.

Writer Lee Rene, The Wild Rose Press author of
Desiree Broussard, Death on Crimson Sails, Mitzi of the Ritz

A creepy, *emotionally charged chiller*, The Embalmer explores heavy themes: death, loss, evil, spirituality…but Wyckoff manages to bring a fun and snappy energy to the story. There are moments of grim horror and emotional agony, but you'll find hope and friendship too. And most of all, the humanity of people driven into despair but finding their way back.

Peter Laws, author of *The Frighteners and Matt Hunter novel series,* **Minister of Creepy Cove Community Church**

CONTENTS

"Once a cockroach, always a cockroach."

-Brae Wyckoff

"One, two, Freddy's coming for you
Three, four, better lock your door
Five, six, grab your crucifix
Seven, eight, gonna stay up late
Nine, ten, never sleep again."

-A Nightmare on Elm Street

CHAPTER 1
THE ANGEL KILLER

THE HEAVYSET MAN, down on one knee, gazed into the night sky, framed by surrounding trees. Closing his eyes, he took a deep breath. "A storm is comin'." He looked back down at his work, "Best get you on your way, little one."

Situated off the path in the community park, he cleared the vegetation out of his way. Eucalyptus trees mixed with pine created a pleasant aroma. There was moisture in the air, a pre-rain indicator. The man's belly was exposed, fat drooping over his belted pants, as he bent over his latest victim. Thunder rumbled in the background as the knife in his right-hand cut into the flesh, and his left hand guided the loose skin to his desired location.

"There, free now." He stood to assess his work. "You're an angel, so beautiful." His head tilted sideways a tad, his face scrunched, "Wait, your wing. It's not right."

He knelt back down, grabbed hold of the six-year-old child's shoulder to lift it up a few inches. His knife sliced an inch more of the loose skin hanging from his exposed back. He laid the boy back down. Tugged the skin taut and then stood. The frail child looked radiant in his eyes.

"That's it. You're ready. Be free."

The man, in his forties, grinned. His cheeks were pudgy, his five-o-clock shadow thick, his brown wavy misshapen hair looked like he had cut it himself. His beige collared shirt had his name stitched, "Steven Murdock" below the San Diego County parks logo.

Lying on the ground was the six-year-old boy that he abducted earlier today. The child was naked. A simple cloth covering lay over his privates. The boy's skin from his back was cut and stretched out as makeshift wings to resemble an angel. His eyes were open, staring lifelessly up into the night sky. His pale skin almost glowed in the dark moonless night.

The pitter-patter of rain began. He said, "It is finished. Today you will be with him in Paradise."

Morning came, and a jogger discovered the body. Soon the media swarmed while the police took control of the area with yellow caution tape. The sound of the tape unrolled, wrapped around a tree, and secured to another faded away. Reporters clicked their high-speed cameras incessantly to capture any part of the gruesome display. More onlookers arrived. Officers repeatedly ordered the gathering crowd to back away. Behind the yellow tape and off to the side, the jogger was questioned. The cop wrote down every word as he recalled his story.

The homicide unit arrived. Two men exited the black unmarked Ford Crown Vic with tinted windows. Long trench coats, one brown, one black, draped down to the tops of their shiny shoes. They ducked under the yellow tape; eyes focused on what's ahead. These men had seen the worst, the most gruesome homicides. But when a child was murdered and displayed in such an evil act of violence, it forced them to suppress their thoughts of vengeance when they finally found the murderer.

One held a hand over his mouth and gave an uneasy squint. The other leaned down closer to inspect the body. He looked back at his partner. Their eyes connected.

"It's him for sure," the black trench coat man said as he stood back up. "It's the Angel Killer."

CHAPTER 2
FUCK YOU

FREDDY FOLEY SAT at the bar, taking the first sip of his beer the bartender had just slid over to him. His friend suddenly sidled up, slapping his shoulder, causing Freddy to lurch forward, trying to keep his drink from splashing all over him. He regained himself, "What the fuck?"

"You never could handle your shit, my friend. Relax."

"You're late, George."

George put his six-foot-two, stocky build back to the bar with elbows propped. He surveyed the dimly lit room. "Why do you like this shithole dive so much? I mean, Vista, really? Can anything good come out of Vista? I mean, come on, dude. Out of all of San Diego, couldn't we at least meet down by the beach instead of this fucking place?"

"You know why. Just order a drink."

"Well, I can see why she hated this place." He rolled his eyes and then made contact with the bartender, "I'll have what he's having." The bartender nodded.

George turned and scooted the barstool closer, sitting down. "So, you working tonight?"

"Yeah, I gotta train a couple newbies."

"So, can I watch?"

"Come on, you know the answer."

"Why are you such a bitch to me? You broke tons of rules in High School, but you can't let your best bro sneak in the fucking back door?"

"Dude, this is my career."

George took hold of his beer from the bartender and took a swig, "Ahhhhh!" He looked at his friend then swooped his beer over in front of him, "Cheers, my friend. Thanks for being such a dick."

Freddy clashed his glass against George's while rolling his hazel eyes. They both took another drink. Then there was an awkward silence.

George broke it. "What if I paid you a hundred bucks?"

"No! Now stop asking."

The sound of colliding pool balls echoed in the background, along with 80's rock music filling the room. A TV behind the bar in front of them had the evening news though it was difficult to hear anything.

George scanned the room, beer in hand. "There isn't a chick in this place, man. You brought me to the fucking dead zone."

Freddy glanced behind him, "There's one. Go get her."

George scoffed, "Dude, she's like my mom's age. Wait, I think she is my mom."

"Just shut up."

"I don't know, man, I might be in love. She's got that cougar swagger. Just look at the way she points that fifty-year-old ass like—"

"I don't care about your mom over there."

"Mom? Really? No, this is all about my future bride." George leaned into Freddy's face, "I just have to thank you for bringing me to this wretched hive of scum and villainy." George tried to kiss Freddy's cheek while laughing hysterically.

Freddy pushed him away and shot him a glance. George put his beer down quickly, shot up his hands, open-palmed, "I'm just messing with you, my friend. So, you invited me to this amazing place with the enjoyable smell of day-old vomit and cleaning products, and I'm sure you can't wait to tell me what's on your mind, right?"

Freddy was sullen. His skinny frame hidden under his jean jacket. A few monochromatic tattoos—a mix of childish choices with bold convictions— peeked out under his white shirt neckline. He had short brown hair coiffed into a fohawk.

"Freddy, what is it?" George nudged him.

Freddy didn't look at him, "Just needed a friend is all."

"Dude, why didn't you just say that, but just so you know, I'm not into guys. Great if it is your thing. I just don't swing that way."

Freddy smirked, lifted his beer, "Cheers to that."

They clinked beers again and drank.

George called out to the bartender. "Another round!"

Another hour passed by as they laughed and drank. George said, "What's up, dude? I mean, what's going on inside that skull of yours?" He tapped Freddy's head with his knuckle.

Freddy moved his head away, "Nothing. Just inside my thoughts a lot lately. Thinking."

"Yeah, that's the problem. You need to stop thinking and get back to living. It's been two years, bro."

Freddy looked at him, "You can't just turn some things off and on like that. I wish I could. God knows I've tried."

"I'm sorry, I don't know what you're going through, man. But know this. I'm here for ya."

"She left me, dude. She just fucking left." He shook his head. "How could she do that?"

George put a hand on his friend's shoulder, "It's fucked up, man. She just couldn't handle her shit. It's not your fault."

"Isn't it?"

"Come on. The whole thing is fucked up. It's not her fault or yours. It just happened."

"I'm fucking spinning in my thoughts, man. I can't get it out of my head. Was there something I missed? Why us? Why anybody?"

"Let's not talk about it. You get all crazy when we do. Instead, why don't we talk about the time we first met?"

Freddy didn't respond. He took another sip of his beer.

"You want another one?"

"No, I gotta get going soon for work."

"It wasn't a fucking question, bro. Bartender, another round."

Freddy smirked and shook his head. He said under his breath, "I could have sworn that was a question."

"I'm sorry, did you say something?"

No response.

"Okay, so anyway, it was that 'Slick Rick' fuck. You remember that dude? What a jackass. So there you were all pathetic in your little underoos in the gym locker room."

"It wasn't underoos," Freddy laughed. "Oh, my God."

"Dude, it's my fucking story. So there you were all pathetic and shit, as this monster with his hideous bulging forehead, do you remember that?" George laughed. "His head was like that movie, The Mask, all bulging and shit. So anyway, there he was with his white towel all rolled up with the tip watered, getting ready to snap you again. You had blood oozing down your leg from the first crack he took at you. Then what happened?"

Freddy looked at George but didn't respond.

"This is when you say, 'George, my hero showed up and saved my scrawny ass.'"

Freddy repeated in slow motion with a patronizing monotone voice, "George, my hero showed up and saved me."

"It was 'saved my scrawny ass', by the way. You're not that good with lines, but yeah, I saved your ass. The look on Slick Rick's face when I came around the corner and told him to 'Fuck off!' was priceless. I think he peed a little. Just a guess."

"Oh, thank you, great one." Freddy started rubbing George's biceps and shoulders, bulging under his slim-fit black Marc Anthony shirt. "You saved me."

"Stop it! You know that freaks me out. But I could change my mind with a few more beers. Not really any other action at this dump."

"There's always your mom over there."

Both laughed and took another drink. Freddy slowly lowered his glass from his face. His gaze fixated on something in front of him. George followed his look.

Freddy yelled, "Hey, bartender! Turn it up!"

The wiry bartender grabbed the remote and cranked up the volume enough to hear over the background noises of the bar. A few people around them also silenced their talking.

"San Diego is on high alert once again. The murderer known as The Angel Killer struck last night in Del Mar. This makes his twelfth victim to date, with the first body discovered twenty years ago in the small town of Jamul. We go live to San Dieguito County Park, where Steve Price is on the scene. Steve, this is horrific. Please tell us what's going on and if any arrests have been made."

"Thank you, Barbara Lee. No arrests have been made, and there are no suspects in this ongoing serial killing spree. Another, still unnamed, child was apparently abducted and brought here, where he was murdered. We don't know if he was actually killed here or somewhere else. It is too graphic to talk about on the news, but the murder was clearly committed by the person identified as the Angel Killer. He left his trademark message, staging this child the same way he has displayed all of the children he has killed. It is truly a sad day in San Diego. Two years ago was the last killing, a little girl named Evelyn Foley in the city of Vista. The police have little to go on. The rain washed away most, if not all, of the evidence, but that didn't stop them from scouring the area. Behind me is the caution tape cordoning off the area where the body was discovered this morning at 6:13 am by a jogger on the trail. That jogger is Mark Lunez, and here is what he had to say earlier."

"I just couldn't believe it at first. It was like a bad dream. No, a nightmare. I will never be able to remove the image of that poor kid from my mind."

"There you have it, Barbara," said Steve Price. "The twelfth child in this twenty-year-long murder rampage. We will have more information for our viewers as it gets released. This is truly a tragic moment and a wound that won't heal until they catch whoever is doing this in our beloved San Diego County. Barbara, back to you."

Shaking her head in disgust, "Thank you, Steve. Wow, this is not an easy news night for any of us. We do know that the victim was a Caucasian boy, approximately six-years-old. We will get you more information as it becomes available. Again, there is no suspect at this time. Authorities are asking for anyone with information to contact them directly."

Freddy suddenly stood, knocking over the barstool. It clattered and rolled on the ground. He dropped his glass of beer, and it shattered. Pointing at the TV, he yelled, "Fuck you, Angel Killer! You killed my little girl! Fuck you!"

CHAPTER 3
WHY DO CHILDREN HAVE TO DIE?

THE ONLY SOUND was the jukebox playing Bon Jovi, 'Wanted Dead or Alive,' as all the patrons in the bar froze in silence. Freddy backed away, bumping into George's "mom" by the pool table. He turned and stumbled out of the building. Slowly, people began to murmur, and the crack of the billiards started up again. George threw a hundred-dollar bill toward the bartender then sprinted outside after his friend.

"Freddy!"

Freddy didn't turn as he fumbled for his keys in his pocket. The car alarm beeped as it was disarmed, and he opened the door.

"Freddy! Wait, man! Don't drive like this!"

He looked hard at George, "I'm sorry. I just can't." He slumped into his white 2016 Kia Rio. The engine started before he closed his door. The lights blared on, and he took off. He watched in his rearview mirror as George's arms flew up in frustration. He saw George pull out his cell phone.

Freddy's cell came to life, flashing caller ID, Bestman. He ignored it. The phone lit up again. This time he answered. "George, I'm sorry, man. I just can't take this anymore." Freddy turned right onto Emerald and then entered the 78 Freeway West.

"Dude, don't blow a gasket. Take some deep breaths. Let me meet you somewhere until you calm down."

"It's okay. I'm just going to work and will sit in the fridge."

"Okay, okay, yeah, that's great. Yeah, let's just talk until you get there."

"It happened again, George. Two fucking years, man. I just can't handle this."

"I know, I know. It's okay."

"It's not okay!"

"Okay, bad choice of words. It's fucked up, I know. I'm with you, bro."

"Why do children have to die, George?"

"I can't answer that. I, I don't know. It's fucked up. This dude has some serious karma coming to him."

"Karma?! What the fuck is that? I want justice, not karma. That's what's wrong in this world, people believing in religion like this nut job hacking kids up. He killed my little girl, George!"

"Yeah, man, I know. Just focus on driving, my friend. Just pretend I'm sitting in the passenger seat talking with you. I'm with you."

"George, did you know my dad never called me after Eve died? He never called. What a complete fucking asshole. What kind of dad is that?"

"The fucked-up kind."

"Get out of the fucking way!" Freddy yelled.

George heard tires squealing in the background. "Okay, dude, just slow down a bit. You are probably coming up to your exit."

"I know where I'm fucking going!"

"Okay, right, yeah. Got it. So, yeah, your dad is a piece of shit, man."

Freddy refocused as he took the El Camino Real exit. Having just enough room to fit between cars waiting at the light, he sped past then cut in front of them, making a right turn. People honked, but he paid no attention to them. Fortunately for everyone, the next light was green as he accelerated.

"Freddy? You there?"

"Yeah, I, I got to go, man. I'll call you later. I'm almost at work now."

"Wait, Freddy, I—" The call ended.

Freddy was a mile away from work. He began to slow the engine down and breathed evenly. He pulled into the parking lot. Parked. Turned off the car. Got out and headed into work, passing the sign that read "Pinewood Memorial Park and Mortuary".

He punched in the security code at the back entrance. Bold red letters stated AUTHORIZED PERSONNEL ONLY on the metal door. The red light turned green, unlocking the heavily bolted entry. He pulled it open and entered. Lights automatically engaged as he stepped into the employee kitchen. The room had a single square table with four cheap, plastic chairs. A refrigerator, microwave, and Keurig lined the far right side, while storage cabinets lined the other two. The room had an insane asylum look and feel to it with its creepy black and white checkered flooring, white cabinets, and a dented door on the fridge. That was courtesy of a disgruntled employee Freddy had to let go a year ago. The microwave light flickered inside, regardless if it was heating anything or not. This place somehow brought Freddy some comfort. He felt at home. This was his domain.

He pulled out his cell and quickly texted George, IM GOOD. AT WORK.

A response chimed in, AWESOME. CALL YOU TOMORROW.

Freddy slid his phone back into his jean pocket and headed into a dark corridor. The lights ignited when the motion sensors caught his movement. He glanced to the right. A door labeled "Embalming Room" was shut. He turned left. A video camera hung above the portal. Freddy saluted the camera, entering the door labeled "Garage". Inside was the sweet smell of fuel, formaldehyde, and a faint smell of rotting meat. A black hearse was parked with the license plate PW RIP immediately in front of him. Behind the hearse, barrels of embalming fluid lined the back wall. Several steel tables clustered in the middle. Some of them had broken wheels waiting for repair.

Freddy made his way to the large gray door labeled "Storage". He popped the door open and cold air cascaded out. A light blinked on. Inside were several bodies. He went to the back of the refrigeration unit, put his back to the wall, and slid down to his butt, knees propped up, releasing a sigh of relief. He closed his eyes and inhaled deeply, exhaling slowly. It was peaceful here. This was the place he often used to cool down, literally, and figuratively.

He opened his eyes. Five bodies covered by white sheets laid on stainless steel lab tables. Three to his right, two to his left. Three of them would be embalmed tonight with the newbies. He checked his phone. It was 10:14 pm. They would arrive at 11. He put his phone away and rested his head back, closing his eyes.

Opening them again, he stared ahead. A blank look. His eyes drifted to the closest table, and he focused on the scratches on the outside frame.

Stainless steel brought him peace. It was something he was used to. He had worked around autopsy tables for over fifteen years. At the age of eight, he knew he would be a mortician. That was when he saw his first body, at his grandfather's open casket funeral. The memory flooded his mind. He had sneaked into the back room before the service. He remembered the smell of cleaning solutions, but it wasn't a normal smell. Whatever it was, he liked it.

He later found out it was Spic and Span mixed with death.

Freddy's dad placed his hand on his shoulder as he stared, mesmerized by the look on his grandfather's face. Freddy called his grandpa, Bapah, something he had called him since he first started talking. Freddy didn't flinch and continued to stare.

Dad said, "He is in a better place, son."

"Where is that?"

"Anyplace but here."

Freddy looked up at him. His eyes were dark. He could tell he had been crying. Dad then knelt down while grabbing Freddy's shoulders to line up with his.

"Son, there is nothing in this world. Only death. Death is everyone's future. Don't ever forget that. There is nothing beyond it. Don't listen to anyone who says different."

He turned him back to see his grandfather, "Take a good look at what awaits everyone in this world. We are born, we live the best we can, and then we die. That is it. That is all there is."

Freddy heard his dad slowly walking away and heard his words in the back of his mind, *"That is all there is."*

From that moment on Freddy never believed in God, not any god. It was all a sham. Something made up to help people cope with the inevitable. They needed a crutch to lean on because the pain of loss was too much for them to bear.

Freddy relaxed again, taking deep breaths, and looked at the covered bodies. "You guys have it easy now. No more problems, no more pain, no more suffering." He stood up and uncovered the face of the body closest to him on his right. It was a male looking to be in his late seventies. His long stringy hair was a greasy white. Face shriveled, wrinkles galore. Teeth jacked up. Most likely a former meth addict from the hippy days.

"If only you could talk, my friend." He waited for a response. Nothing. "What's out there? What's beyond? Just darkness? Seems lonely, but I imagine it's peaceful." He paused as he caressed the decedent's cheek. "If only I could talk to Eve. Can you give her a message? Can you tell her that her daddy loves her and misses her? Can you ask her for my forgiveness? It's my fault she's dead. I wasn't there for her. I looked away for just a minute." His heart began to race as the memory of losing his daughter that Saturday afternoon at the park playground came flooding back. He was sitting and watching her play. His wife sat by his side. They began to talk. Eve yelled from the playground, "Watch me, mommy and daddy!"

"Yes, baby. So good!" he yelled in response, but not really paying attention. Mommy and Daddy were having marital problems.

Counseling wasn't working. The counselor wanted to talk about God as his wife was a Christian, but Freddy was far from that. Considered an atheist as the world would label him these days. Freddy didn't like labels and instead made disrespectful statements, "I'm just an asshole like the rest of the people in the world. The only difference is I know there is nothing after death. All others just believe in fairy tales to help them cope. No different than a drug addict."

Then Eve was gone. Nowhere to be found. Freddy and Jenny searched and searched. Two days later, her body was found at South Buena Vista Park at 5:44 am. Three miles away from where he last saw her at the Vista Calavera Park. On April 30th, 2014, Evelyn Foley, age 5, became the eleventh Angel Killer murder victim. That was almost two years ago.

"It's almost your birthday, Eve," Freddy whispered. "Seven, wow, you are growing up so fast." He looked down at the old man cadaver and brushed his cheek. "June 10th, 2009, is the first time we met face to face. You melted my heart that day, sweetheart. More than anyone or anything." He paused as his voice began to clench with emotion. "I'm sorry. So, so, sorry. Please forgive me." He broke, then planted his face onto the chest of the old man and sobbed.

CHAPTER 4
THE NEWBIES

AFTER WASHING HIS face, Freddy sat in his office to prepare for the trainees to arrive. It was a simple room. Desk, lamp, computer, a fake plant in the corner that his ex-wife gave him to add some color. The most prominent thing as you entered was the framed movie poster of the original *A Nightmare on Elm Street*. It was signed by the actor Robert Englund. But the crown jewel was kept in a glass-domed case on the corner of his mahogany desk. It was a movie replica of Freddy Krueger's clawed glove. The leather strap was signed with an added bonus from the actor, "1-2 Coming For You".

A knock at the door jarred him from his stare at the bladed glove. "Come in!"

The door opened and an Asian male in his early twenties stood in the entry. Behind him was a young woman with multi-colored purple, red, and orange hair with dreads starting to form while the rest of her hair was all over the place. Freddy resisted judging them right off the bat. He had been surprised by many new employees in the past.

The Asian kid sprang to life, hastily entering and enraptured by the movie prop, "Oh my God, it is true. You totally have Freddy's claw in your office."

Now, Freddy was ready to judge. "Yes, by all means, come in and have a seat."

The girl walked in chewing bubble gum and blowing a bubble that popped loudly. She looked like someone from the movie set of The Breakfast Club. Specifically, Ally Sheedy.

Freddy said, "Rule #1: No chewing gum."

She paused mid-chew, stared at him briefly with her dark lined eyes, and then spat it out into her hand looking around for trash. Freddy leaned over, grabbed his wastebasket, and held it up to her. She threw it away.

"Hello boys and girls, my name is—"

"Freddy Foley," the young man said. He smiled in the awkward silence and then got fidgety in his chair.

"Rule #2: Let the teacher talk and don't interrupt."

The young man nodded.

"Great, as I was saying, my name is Frederick Foley, but you can call me Freddy. I will be conducting your first teaching on embalming tonight."

The girl added, "I did extensive embalming in school so this is more of a formality that we need checked off the list, right?"

"Rule #3: I don't care about any of your schooling. These are actual decedents who will be viewed by loved ones. I will show you the true standards we need to uphold for our clients. Which is way more extreme than your classroom environment."

"Yeah, to win awards and stuff," the young man said.

"What is your name?" Freddy asked with a stretched polite tone.

"Um-"

"It's Um?"

"No, it's..." he faltered.

"You don't remember or you don't know?"

"It's Joshua," he said flustered.

Freddy looked at the girl. She responded, "Cyndi with a 'y' and an 'i', you know, like Cyndi Lauper. People just call me Cyn, though."

Freddy raised an eyebrow at her explanation. "Okay, Joshua and

Cyn, Rule #4:it is not about our performance but about our decedent. Understand?"

They both nodded. Freddy stared at them hard. "The last rule, rule #5, is the most important of them all. It's the one rule that most of the new employees just can't handle and they end up quitting."

Joshua gulped, "Quitting? Really?"

"Yes."

"What is it?" Cyndi asked.

"Rule #5: I like my coffee black." He held the serious tone and stare for what seemed like an eternity before erupting into laughter.

The held breaths of the new employees let go and half-baked smiles came out.

"I'm just fucking with you guys. Hey, it is nice to meet you both." He reached out his hand to shake theirs. Both of them began to relax but with nervous giggles.

Freddy stood, "Okay, let's embalm. All I ask is for professionalism. No joking about the deceased person you are working on, but everyone else is fair game. Sound good?"

They stood and smiled.

"Okay, right this way." Freddy led them out of his office and to the left. The embalming room was the next door. The old man he had met in the refrigerator earlier was in the room waiting for them. There were two embalming stations but only one body. Nothing was prepped. He wanted to oversee the new employees run through the steps and watch their progress with guidance along the way as needed. Freddy did have one surprise for them, however, but he would wait until the end to reveal that. He waved them in.

"Okay, as you can see, we already have Mr. Reynolds ready for us, head lifted onto the block. Let's get our PPE going. Everything you need is to your right. Goggles, face masks, rubber overalls, boots, gloves, aprons, the works. Let's suit up."

After several minutes of putting on their gear, Joshua and Cyn were ready to start. Each student stood on either side of Mr. Reynolds.

Freddy positioned himself at the head of the table. The cadaver was fully naked with a sheet covering his privates. His skin was almost translucent under the fluorescent lighting.

Freddy grabbed a chart dangling on a chain, "Mr. Reynolds was 76 years old. Died of a heart attack two days ago. Family viewing is this weekend. Okay," he let the chart dangle back down, "what is the first step?"

"Eye caps?" Joshua pointed out.

"I would say we wash the body first," Cyn chimed.

"Neither, we check the vitals. Most students miss this part. You don't want your decedent suddenly waking up on you. Not that he will. It's more of a formality, but a necessary step to log if you want to cover your own ass." Joshua and Cyn exchanged glances.

Joshua said, "Has anyone hopped up off the table before?"

Freddy paused, "Like I said, more of a formality in case anything legal were to come up. Prosecutors would have a field day with any discrepancies in procedures. So, the first step is always checking vital signs to prevent premature burial. Embalmers need to check for clouded corneas, lividity, rigor mortis, and a pulse in the carotid or radial artery."

The students did as instructed, seemingly comfortable with all the steps. But at the same time, realizing this particular point wasn't expressed as important in the classroom environment.

"Okay, good," Freddy continued, "One of you said eye caps, and the other said wash. You can go either route. I find that if we put the eye caps in now before washing and something goes wrong, you could damage the eyelids which will make extra steps when getting make-up ready. What's the most prominent thing family will see at the viewing?"

Simultaneously the students said, "The face."

"Yes, so let's begin by getting Mr. Reynolds cleaned up."

The students pulled out the hose sprayer and got the stainless-steel bed elevated and tilted for water to drain. Cyn began spraying while Joshua lathered the cadaver with soap. Suds and contaminants began to cascade down into the funneled drain. Splashes of water sprayed up into their protective face shields. They were all in the area termed the "Splash Zone".

Cyndi swabbed the eyes, nose, and mouth with disinfectant, then followed by rinsing with a jet of water. The mouth gave a hollow echo as the water filled, then cascaded over his cheeks on either side. This was where regular folk would gag on impulse, as if they were drowning themselves, just by watching this take place. This was a business where one must look at the deceased as just an empty shell that once housed the deceased person. It was as if they were now getting the vehicle cleaned up for the next soul to be invited in but alas, one soul to one body. No, embalming was preparing the vehicle for its final departure six feet below ground.

"Okay, next step? What is it?"

Cyn said, "Secure the face."

"Good. Proceed."

Before any incision is made, embalmers need to set the features of the deceased. Freddy pulled out a picture of Mr. Reynolds that the family provided so the students could see how he looked alive. The eyes were posed using an eye-cap, which keeps the eyes shut and in a "natural" expression. The mouth was then set by wiring the jaw shut, suturing the lips and gums, and then an adhesive was used to make the expression look as relaxed and natural as possible. Freddy continued to supervise their work, pointing out little corrections or commenting, "Looking good."

Joshua started the final shave of the face of the cadaver. Freddy said, "Be careful to not give Mr. Reynold's any nicks. It is hard to repair the damage as the skin doesn't heal any longer. Make sure to have the one razor, one body rule in place. Always throw away the razor after you are done." Joshua and Cyn kept working, but their body language was receiving the information flowing from Freddy Foley.

Freddy hid his underlying thoughts behind his work. He kept focus on the instructions he gave, the process of embalming a body.

Joshua said, "I wonder if Mr. Reynolds ever thought about his last shave. Bet he didn't guess he would get one additional shave after that one."

Cyn didn't respond as she was getting the fluid tank ready with the chemicals to be introduced into the cadaver's circulatory system and replace the blood.

"Pop quiz," Freddy announced, "What are the three words we don't use referring to the body?"

Joshua chimed in with no hesitation like he was a robot regurgitating programmed information, "Stiff, corpse, cadaver."

"And Cyn, what are the three acceptable terms in place of those?"

Also, without hesitation, "Decedent, remains, or Mr. Reynolds."

Freddy nodded his approval, "Okay, we have cleaned the outside. Now let's get Mr. Reynolds all cleaned out inside."

"Alright," Joshua clapped with a big grin on his face, "my favorite part. Just like the frat parties in college. Pump in the alcohol."

"Okay, Joshua. Go ahead and take the lead, and Cyn will assist."

"Alright!" Joshua settled in position on Mr. Reynolds' right side. "Scalpel." He placed his open palm out to receive. Nothing was given to him. He looked at Cyndi, who stared at him.

"Really?" she said.

"Sorry, I always wanted to say that."

She placed the scalpel in his hand. He responded, "Thanks."

At this point, if she was still chewing gum, Freddy imagined she would have blown a bubble and popped it in Joshua's face while throwing one of her hips out to lean on with a 'whatever' attitude. In this industry, embalmers came in many shapes, sizes, and attitudes.

"Okay," Joshua said, "We're now in search of the carotid artery." His statement sounded like he was the one teaching a class of onlookers. He cut a short two-inch lengthwise slit in the man's neck. No blood flowed out. Joshua stuck his finger into the open pocket. It sounded like rummaging your fingers into spaghetti. After some probing, he found and pulled forth the artery, quickly severing it with his blade.

The artery looked like pink rubber stretched outside of Mr. Reynold's pasty neck.

Cyndi smiled and said, "Reminds me of my bubble-gum."

Joshua took the cannula from Cyn's grasp and inserted it with ease. The device was connected by a length of tubing to a canister of prepared embalming fluid.

"Fire it up," Joshua said.

Cyn leaned over and turned the machine on. Within minutes, the man's face began to look rejuvenated. The students massaged the body to allow the proper flow of the fluids through the circulatory system. The fluid rehydrated the tissues, filling out sunken cheeks and wrinkles. The color came back, replacing pasty white with pink skin because the fluid contained red coloring agents. After several minutes of the gurgling sounds of the fluid and machine, the transformation was complete. The dead almost looked alive, just sleeping.

Freddy said, "Well, Mr. Reynolds just got a complete makeover. Seventy-six to mid-fifties. Not too bad. Okay, what's next?"

Cyn said, "Aspirate gas and fluids built up in the organs."

"Proceed."

Joshua began looking around the counter and a couple drawers. He turned to Freddy, "Uh, where are the A/V plugs at?"

Freddy softly smiled and said, "Oh, I forgot to tell you that our A/V plugs are on backorder."

"What?" Joshua scoffed. "Are you kidding?"

"It appears you need to do this one the old-fashioned way. Always good to be prepared when you don't have the products you need."

"So, what? Is this part of our training or something?" Joshua asked.

Cyn said, "Just get over it. It's no big deal suturing the anus."

Freddy turned and began to walk away, "We don't want any leakage to wick into the funeral clothing. It's an awful mess. Finish up the decedent with make-up and final clean up. I'll come back to review your work."

CHAPTER 5
THE CALL

I T WAS 3:14 am. Freddy Foley sat in his car, staring at the light fog rolling in over the grassy park. Only one lamp next to the bathroom a hundred yards away illuminated the area, giving off a creepy, movie set aura. Freddy had been sitting in his car for the last fifteen minutes in complete silence. This is where he drove to, no hesitation, right after finishing work with the new Pinewood employees.

A playground, not just any playground, but *the* playground where his daughter last played, stood resolute before him like a memorial. The faded colors of the red and blue plastic tubes she had climbed through and the slides she had conquered at the age of four were frozen in place in his mind. It was like he was watching a movie. He could see himself and his wife on the park bench and all the ghostlike images of children in the background playing and running. His daughter, Eve, blonde hair frazzled from running around, stood still at the bridge leading to the largest slide, watching mommy and daddy arguing—kids ran by her in all directions oblivious to her concern.

Freddy imagined his blue-eyed daughter climbing down and slowly making her way to the bathroom, peering back occasionally, while mommy and daddy were unaware. He watched her ghostlike image fade into the fog. She was never seen alive again. Tears rolled from his eyes.

His voice cracked as he choked out, "I'm sorry, Eve. I'm so, so, sorry."

Freddy lowered his forehead into his steering wheel. His face contorted in the pure pain of his loss. "Whyyyyy?" he cried out over and over. "She's my baby. Whyyy?"

Minutes passed. He settled into his seat, motionless, until jarred to consciousness by his buzzing phone. He opened his messages.

"Jenny?" he whispered in surprise.

It read HEARD NEWS TODAY. THINKING ABOUT YOU.

Freddy didn't text back. He called.

She answered, "Freddy?"

"Yeah, I'm here." He stuttered a bit, "I'm, I'm at the park, Jenny."

"Now?"

"Jenny, I don't know. I can't. I just can't deal with this."

"It's okay, Freddy. I'm struggling too."

"Why aren't we still together, Jenny? I miss you."

"You know why. Freddy, I, I just couldn't. I blame myself more than anyone."

There was silence for a second.

"Jenny, that sick fuck killed another kid."

She didn't respond. But he heard sniffling on the other end.

"He was six years old. The police can't find this fucking guy. No one has seen anything." He paused, "I can't find him either."

"Freddy, come on. You said you had stopped."

He scoffed, "What, it's not like anyone is doing anything, and kids are dying. What else do I have?"

More silence. But he knew she was saying inside, *"You can't bring her back."*

Jenny said, "I'm coming out there to visit my parents in November for dad's birthday."

"Yeah, that's cool. I won't push you to see me."

"No, Freddy, I do want to see you. That's why I'm telling you. Maybe you can come to the party. Mom and dad would love to see you."

"Yeah, maybe." He took a deep breath and exhaled. "It's tough to be around anyone who knew Eve."

"I know, but our counselors say it's the best thing we can do to help us get through it. I know we ended our marriage, I mean, I did, but we all still need to get through this together somehow. Mom and dad are hurting too. They lost their granddaughter."

Freddy opened his car door and stepped out into the cool, wet air. He strolled toward the playground, one hand in his pocket, the other holding his cell to his ear.

"I wish you were here, Jenny."

Silence.

"Freddy," she paused, "I know we haven't talked in a while but what I want to tell you has to be in person. I can't do it over the phone."

Freddy bypassed her comment and spurted out, "I love you, Jenny. I always will."

She was quiet at first, then said, "Um, yeah, that's what we need to talk through. Our feelings. It's not fair to either one of us. I just can't do this over the phone. Let's connect when I come out in a few months. Okay?"

"Yeah, sure."

A male voice, garbled in the background, but Freddy clearly heard, "Honey?"

Jenny fired off, "I've got to go." Then hung up.

Freddy pulled the cell phone away and saw the blinking message- 'Call Ended'. He looked up to find himself on the same bench where they had argued. The same bench they had seen their little girl alive for the last time. The same bench he had visited alone many times in the last two years. And now the same bench where he found out Jenny had another man in her life.

A door slammed, startling him. It was on the other side of the bathroom.

"Hello?" he called out.

It was peculiarly quiet. Then a silhouette of a head peered around the corner. The person called back, "Hello? Parks and Rec doing some cleaning."

Freddy's racing heart slowed down, "Sorry, just startled me. Wasn't expecting someone out here."

A large man came into view below the lamp. Heavyset, short, keys dangling on his belt loop, khaki pants with matching beige city park issued collared shirt, and a hat. He couldn't make out any details of the face.

The man responded, "Same here. Wasn't expecting anyone out here so late. Couldn't sleep, heh?"

"Yeah, something like that," Freddy said. "You have a good night, or should I say a good morning."

"Thanks, you do the same." The worker went back to his cleaning— taking the trash out of the outside cans and throwing the tied-up black bag to the side where he would grab it later to haul away.

Freddy watched for a second, then turned and headed back to his car. It was time to go home.

CHAPTER 6
THE GIVER

A WEEK HAD PASSED since Jeffrey Sellik, the now identified murdered boy, was found. Headlines across the nation read 'The Infamous Angel Killer Strikes Again' or 'Murdered Children, Is It God's Plan?' Freddy kept himself busy at work and even took on removal of bodies from hospitals and homes to keep himself occupied. This recent event brought all the memories to the surface. It was as if a scab had been ripped off. He understood the trauma the parents were going through. The constant media hype at their residence all day and night, and how everything important to the world suddenly becomes meaningless. As much as he tried to busy himself with more work, in the end, there was no escape from his own mind. Thoughts of his daughter Eve and his ex-wife, Jenny, with another man, devoured him. How could he blame her? It had been almost two years.

Freddy stood in front of a large glass window overlooking the Pacific Ocean. Waves crashed directly below him. The sun was setting and seagulls perched on the bluff taking in the final rays. He could smell the salt air.

"How do you keep these windows so clean?" Freddy called out.

George Casey, his longtime friend, answered. "Well," he said nonchalantly as he approached with a couple of drinks, "all I do is put on my Ironman suit with a squeegee in hand. Voila." George handed Freddy his drink.

"How did you get this place again?"

"Well, that's an interesting story. Long story short, I won it in a Sabaac hand on the planet Tatooine. Cheers," George grinned while holding his drink out for the traditional clash.

Freddy clinked his glass, "Okay, guess it's one of those nights."

"And what kind of night is that?"

"The night where you don't want to talk about something that you don't want to talk about kind of night."

"Matter of fact, it is. I don't really want to talk about windows or buying fucking homes, my friend."

"So, what do ya want to talk about then?" he resigned.

George set his drink down on the white marble-topped coffee table. A decorative knick-knack of a blue crystal wave rested on top. His friend had the largest white leather couch Freddy had ever seen. It seemed to stretch out fifteen million feet long and wrapped around to a recliner sectional for giants. George plopped into the couch, pointed at Freddy, and said, "I'm a fucking giver, my friend. Do you know that?"

Freddy stared at him and took a sip without a word.

George continued, "I love giving things. I love helping others. It just makes me feel all kinds of...I don't know, all kinds of fucking goodness inside."

Freddy laughed, "Fucking goodness inside? You kind of remind me of James Spader right now the way you're talking."

"Yeah, whatever, I'm sharing my feelings bro, so don't mess with my flow."

"Okay, proceed."

"So last week, I picked up this hitchhiker down in Encinitas along the 101."

Freddy pulled his drink away, "You did what?"

"Just listen. I picked up this dude. Typical surfer guy. Turns out his car wouldn't start over at Swami's. Anyway, long story short, he needed to get home to help his mom, who just got the news she has cancer. I'm like, "Dude, my mom had cancer, and she fucking beat it." I totally encouraged this guy all the way back home. He was so thankful. I couldn't stop thinking about this guy. His name is Pete. So, I just got off the phone with my attorney to set up funds going to his mom for cancer treatments and whatever else she needs. I think it was some type of divine appointment."

Freddy raised an eyebrow. George caught his look and responded, "I know you don't believe in that shit, and maybe you're right."

"Maybe?"

"And maybe you're fucking wrong, dude. Anyway, I'm stoked to have helped Pete and his mom, Maurene."

Freddy relented and said, "That's amazing. Truly amazing."

"So, yeah, there you have it. I love helping people."

"Yes, you do. I can't think of anyone you have denied help to...well, maybe one."

"Who?"

"You didn't want to help——"

"I don't care who you're going to bring up." George's hands shot up, and his face scrunched. "I have something else to talk about, so listen up. Actually, sit your ass down." He pointed to the recliner section.

Irritated, Freddy looked at George hard. He walked to the recliner side of the couch and sat down.

George said, "Okay, I know this week has been a complete cluster fuck for you, and when shit hits the fan, I always say fuck it let's get away."

"'Fuck it, let's get away?'"

"Yeah."

"Okay, get away where?"

George smiled, pulled his cell out of his pocket, slid his finger around on the screen, and handed it to Freddy. "Take a look at this."

Freddy tried to digest what he was reading. It was an email notification for an approved purchase.

"Scroll down. You'll see it."

Freddy did as instructed and quickly realized it was concert tickets for two to see the Hollywood Vampire show. Freddy looked up at George. Surprised.

"Happy fucking birthday!"

Freddy's face scrunched, "It's April, dude. It's not my birthday until October."

"Happy *early* fucking birthday, then. Dude, we're going to New York to see Alice Cooper and his other cohorts. It's going to be epiclessly delicious."

Freddy smiled, "Epiclessly?"

"Yeah, just made up a new word. It will be in the dictionary soon. You know what I fucking mean, dude. So, what do you think?"

Freddy was mesmerized, "I can't believe this. Are you serious?"

"Dude, does George not come through or what?" He stood up, threw his arms up high, and yelled, "I'm a fucking giverrrrr!"

Freddy laughed, "Yes, you are."

George plopped back down, grabbed his drink, and sipped. "Concert is May 24th, so get the time off."

"Yeah, no problem. I can't believe this. It's next month. That's crazy."

"It's gonna get fucking crazy. It's in New York. I booked us first class all the way, baby."

Freddy pensively said, "So let me know how much you need me to pitch in."

George froze in place, raised an eyebrow, and said, "Did you just fucking insult me?"

"No."

"Yeah, you did. Dude, it's a gift so just accept it. I have a ton of fucking money from my biz, bro, so there you have it. Just ride the wave."

Freddy got up and hugged George, "Thank you so much. This means the world right now."

"You're welcome. I'm here for you, man. You need a break. We both do."

They separated and gave a high-five. Freddy was astounded, "I can't fucking believe this. We're going to see Alice fucking Cooper next month."

George said, "You realize this is their premiere show, right? Oh yeah, I forgot to tell you we also have VIP backstage passes."

Freddy's mouth fell open, "What!?"

"That's right, I'm a fucking giverrr!"

CHAPTER 7
HOLLYWOOD VAMPIRES

F REDDY STARED AT the ticket he held until his trance was inter-
rupted when the overhead speakers echoed. A calm female voice
announced, "Welcome to San Diego International airport. For
security reasons, please make sure your bags are with you at all times."
The message droned. Freddy tuned it out and continued to stare at his
ticket.

"It's real, bro."

Freddy looked up at George, "I can't believe we're going to meet
Alice Cooper. This is crazy."

George said, "Yeah, man, the Godfather of Shock Rock himself."
His voice went deeper as he amplified his words to sound like the guy
who calls out the boxer's name when they enter the ring, "It's time to
get lit!"

Others waiting gave George scorned looks for being so obnoxious.
George paid them no mind. He was in his own world and didn't care
what others thought. Those who know George understand that he has
the biggest heart.

A male flight attendant at the gate announced, "We will be
pre-boarding flight 4927 to JFK in a few minutes. Please make sure

you have your ticket out so we can get everyone on board with no delays."

George was tall, six-foot-two with a stocky build. He worked out six days a week with one of the trainers that worked with Gerard Butler for the movie *300*. He had thick bristled orangey-blonde hair, which made him stand out in a crowd. He owned his own indoor rock-climbing gym business, aptly named Hang In There. It boasted dozens of locations throughout California, Nevada, and Arizona.

"Freddy, check this out." George lifted his tight-fitting shirt and flexed his stomach. Well-defined muscles flared to life, revealing an eight-pack. "Pure perfection, baby." His perfect straight white teeth gleamed as he gloated. "Bet you haven't embalmed anything as beautiful as this."

Freddy laughed, "I'm like the dead. We tell no tales."

George leaned over from his chair and said, "That's why only the living get laid, my friend. The dead have no game."

First-class flight from San Diego to JFK. Private limo from the airport to the hotel. This was just the first day. They arrived Sunday evening. The concert was Tuesday night, and their departure back home was scheduled for Thursday morning.

Hollywood Vampire posters were everywhere in the city. The show was sold-out. They had a penthouse suite at Turning Stone Resort and Casino. As a bonus, the hotel gave them $100 each in gambling money. Gambling was only the means to an end—have drinks, flirt with the ladies, and pass the time away before the main event.

George worked out Monday morning and did some remote work in his room. Freddy walked the resort and then ventured out on the streets to get some fresh air. Eventually, they both met for lunch, had a scheduled private massage, and took a nap. Monday night, they hit the casino hard.

George and Freddy connected with two women visiting from Austria. They had a make-out session in the casino bar VIP lounge, played high-stakes poker in the same area, got drunk off their asses, and laughed until they puked in the morning.

Tuesday arrived. They woke up late afternoon after partying all night. Room service came. Reminiscing, Freddy said, "I lost my shirt, literally, I mean, I can't find it. It's gone. It must be somewhere in the casino."

George laughed and then scrunched his face from the hangover, "I think Talia took it as a souvenir. Stranger things have happened. Can you pass me the butter?" George scraped some butter onto his toast and said, "Just another amazing memory that we'll talk about for years to come, my friend."

"George," Freddy's tone was serious, catching his friend before taking a bite of his toast. "Whatever happens, I just want you to know that this time together is more important than any fancy hotel or VIP concert."

George paused for a long second. The opening for a close, transparent moment between friends quickly shut down. "Really, dude, you want to have a moment right now?" He sighed, "Whatever." George saluted with his bread in hand and then took a bite of his toast with a loud crunch. They lounged around and rested before the main event.

They had second-row seats, and doors opened at 6 pm. VIP's didn't have to wait in any line but instead had their own lounge to meet other VIP guests, eat food, laugh, talk, and wait for the show to start.

Not only was it Alice Cooper, but also Joe Perry, Aerosmith guitarist, and Johnny Depp. The band included Stone Temple Pilots bassist Robert DeLeo, drummer Matt Sorum (The Cult, Guns N' Roses), guitarist Tommy Henriksen (Alice Cooper), and multi-instrumentalist Bruce Witkin (from Johnny Depp's group The Kids).

The show officially started at 8:13 pm with an original Depp song called *Raise the Dead*. He was the sex symbol of the night as thousands of girls screamed every time he would open his mouth. Perry, a rock royalty legend, was dressed in deep purple. He seemed to have an endless supply of guitars at his disposal because around 8:30 p.m., Perry smashed his white guitar and threw pieces of it into the crowd. Freddy scored a white splinter as a keepsake and placed it in his pocket after showing George his catch.

Another white guitar appeared in its place, only to be traded for an orange and white Arrow during *Break on Through*, and later, a classic black shredder. He played just as he always had, with razor-sharp licks and even a behind-the-head solo on *Stop Messin' Around*. This rocker gave new meaning to the word legend.

However, the one that stole the stage was Alice himself. At 68, Cooper commanded the stage with vigorous vocals, glam rock swagger, and full "vampire" attire. Lestat style, not sparkles like Edward Cullen. His frilly poet shirt was splattered with blood, and despite wearing both a corset and skintight leather pants, Cooper missed no opportunities to gyrate his hips. George and Freddy did the same. Nothing like a good hip gyration at an Alice Cooper concert.

The night was in every way a tribute to the real Hollywood Vampires. "This is for all my brothers who drank until they couldn't walk," Cooper yelled out to the audience. "I was the only one who walked out."

But there was no bitterness or solemnity to the Hollywood Vampires performance. The tribute was celebratory, with deep respect paid to every fallen rock star's life. "For John," Cooper said, before belting out *Cold Turkey* as hard as he could.

They played nineteen songs and two encore songs. Five-thousand fans went bat-shit all night. They played everything, honoring the rockers who were now gone: The Who, Hendrix, Lennon, Beatles, Zeppelin, Bowie, Doors, and more. Freddy felt like Alice in Wonderland, who fell down the rabbit hole into an alternate universe.

The concert ended a little shy of 10 pm. George and Freddy bounced up and down all night, celebrating every song and singing along. It was an incredible evening.

"Dude, now we get to go backstage!" George yelled.

In unison, they both leaned back with invisible guitars and played lead with tongues hanging out.

They each had backstage passes dangling from lanyards around their necks. Fans whispered their jealousy as they passed by. Security held everyone else back but ushered them through after scrutinizing their credentials. They high fived each other as they walked down the corridor along the stage. More guards pointed the way.

It felt surreal as two people dressed in black suits and wearing sunglasses opened the double doors. Alice Cooper smiled as they walked through. At this point, both George and Freddy didn't remember walking in but instead felt like they were floating in on a cerebral ecstasy high.

"Hey guys, come on in," Alice said.

Freddy thought, *It's Alice fucking Cooper!*

CHAPTER 8
ALICE IN WONDERLAND

S WEATY ROCKERS FROM the concert were scattered amongst twenty other guests who had bought the VIP package. George and Freddy stood in front of Alice Cooper, who still was in his blood-spattered costume and eye make-up. The smell of expensive perfume and rocker sweat ignited Freddy's senses as he locked onto Alice Cooper's blue eyes. He was caught in the celebrity trance like a tractor beam from Star Wars. Freddy had a goofy smile on his face, but he didn't care.

Alice said, "So where you guys from?"

George answered, "We're from San Diego." He pointed at Alice, "Detroit, right?"

Cooper's face lit up, "Yeah, that's right. Man, I love San Diego. Especially those sunsets in La Jolla."

George sparked up, "I live about twenty minutes away."

"Really? That's awesome. So, what're your names?" Alice paused.

"I'm George. This is Freddy."

"It's awesome to meet you guys, and thanks for coming out to our show. It truly means a lot to all of us."

George said, "I can't believe you're thanking us. We're the ones who should be thanking you. We needed an escape from work, and this was a dream come true."

"Oh, wow," Alice Cooper placed his hand over his heart, "that touches my heart, man. Truly."

"Hey, can we get a selfie?" George really wasn't waiting for a response. He got out his cell phone and began lining up the picture. Alice Cooper blared his eyes, stuck out his tongue, and lifted his fingers in the typical *Rock On* salute. Freddy and George had the biggest grins on their faces.

"Hey, one more." Johnny Depp swaggered over, and George took another selfie with all four of them in the picture. Then the other band members showed up for more pictures. They thrived on the attention. VIPs began pulling out their cell phones. They were all waiting for the green light to take pictures, unsure if it would be allowed. George was the match that lit the room up, as always.

After several more photos, one of which was George being held up like a guitar by several band members, including Alice, they began to break off into social clusters once again. The hosts wanted to make sure everyone got their money's worth as each backstage pass cost thousands of dollars.

Alice asked, "So what do you guys do for a living?"

"I own indoor rock-climbing gyms."

"There's money in that?" Alice asked in jest.

"Not as much as sold-out concerts," George responded.

"Keyword is sold-out, my friend."

They laughed. Freddy was nervous. He knew it was his turn to share what he did. His mouth was dry.

"And what about you, Freddy? What do you do?" Alice asked.

"Me? Um, I'm an embalmer."

Alice's eyebrows raised. He wasn't prepared for that one. "An embalmer? Like dead bodies?"

George smiled as Alice nudged him in disbelief.

"Yeah, dead bodies," Freddy said.

"Wow, I don't think I've ever met an embalmer before. Fascinating."

George wrapped his arm around Freddy's neck, his hand draped the other side, "This guy is a fucking genius when it comes to embalming. He's up for embalmer of the year kind of shit. Isn't that right?"

"Really?" Alice said.

Freddy, awkwardly, said, "Yeah, something like that."

"Something like that?" George scoffed, "Dude, truth is, this guy respects the dead so much it's like they're still living."

Alice smirked, "That's amazing. Hey, listen, let's get you introduced to these guys over here," he pointed to his left. Joe Perry and Tommy Henriksen broke away from a husband and wife to join them. Alice said, "I hope to connect later--I've got to meet a few more people. It was truly a pleasure meeting you both. Rock on."

George said, "Thanks, Alice. Rock on, dude."

Freddy smiled and acknowledged him with a low-toned thank you as well. George began hitting it off with the other band members and Freddy continued to smile and try to absorb everything that was happening. He felt like he was in the room but invisible.

The night was incredible. It was hypnagogic. It was fantastic. It was life changing. They met everyone, engaged in small talk, met other superfans, and had some drinks. Freddy noticed Alice Cooper only drank water, but he knew he battled alcoholism. It brought him a bit of peace of mind knowing someone was winning the battle, unlike his dad.

Things wrapped up, and it was time to go. It was 11:30.

George and Freddy were about to walk out when suddenly one of the security guards in sunglasses and black suit came up to them and handed Freddy a note.

"What's this?"

The man didn't respond and left. Freddy looked at George, who shrugged.

"Is this another one of your birthday surprises?" Freddy asked.

George raised his hands in surrender, "Not me, bro. I'm all out. Gave you all I got."

Freddy looked back at the note and opened the folded paper. Handwritten in blue ink, it said, "Freddy, can we talk for a minute in my hotel tomorrow morning? Turning Stone Resort. Room PH4. 8 am." Signed Alice.

George was overlooking the note and said, "Holy shit."

Freddy looked at him, dumbfounded, "Is this for real?"

"Dude, happy fucking birthday to you."

George grabbed Freddy into a right-armed chokehold. They walked out as Freddy pulled himself away, laughing. "I'm not going to be able to sleep now."

George said, "Good, cuz the casino is open all night. Let's go."

CHAPTER 9
THE DIVINE APPOINTMENT

FREDDY TRIED TO wipe the sweat off his hands. Alice Cooper opened the door in a plush white bathrobe and blue pajama bottoms.

"Hey, Freddy. Come on in. I ordered some food for us so let's dive in. I'm starving."

"Thank you," Freddy said timidly, following Alice to the catered food trays on rolling carts. They reminded Freddy instantly of his embalming tables.

"I know you're freaking out," Alice said, "but I just wanted us to have some private time away from all the chaos." He grabbed a plate of food and handed it to Freddy.

"Is it that obvious?" He responded as he took hold of the plate.

"Yeah, well, I've seen worse. People passing out. One person had a heart attack. They're okay, by the way, but it sure freaked me out," he chuckled. He grabbed his plate and walked into the living room area. Freddy followed. He made a mental note to inform George that their room was better than Alice's.

There was yogurt, eggs, bananas, bacon, orange juice, toast, and coffee. It was a spread. His penthouse had a killer view of the surrounding area, but Freddy was so intimidated he couldn't enjoy or even pay attention to too many details. This was crazy. He was having breakfast with a rock legend.

Alice Cooper sat down on the white velvet couch and pointed to the matching chair across from him for Freddy to sit.

"So, listen, Fred, or is it Freddy?"

"Freddy, thanks."

"Freddy, I wanted to talk to you about your profession."

He let out an eternal sigh of relief. This whole time it was all about his work. The visions in his mind throughout the night and early morning suddenly cracked into a thousand pieces. Freddy had mentally committed to going on tour with him.

"Okaaayyy," he slowly responded.

"Yeah, weird, right?" Alice continued, "So I had a friend die recently from surgery. He never woke up after going under. It turns out there might be some negligence on the doctor's part. So my question is, once a body is embalmed, can there still be an autopsy to find out anything?"

Freddy looked at him and said, "Yeah, of course."

"Really? They can still do it?"

"Yeah, but the only issue you'll have is if it relates to blood sampling, 'cause the embalming process eliminates and replaces the fluids."

"Oh, man. Yeah, they need the blood, I'm sure of it."

"What did your friend have surgery for? If you don't mind me asking."

"No, not at all. He had to get a vein in his leg replaced because of blockage issues. He had other ailments going on. He was older, blah, blah, and the two or three doctors he had weren't communicating. They shouldn't have put him under the knife. He just couldn't recover from it." He sighed. "I'm bummed cause I never got to say goodbye."

Freddy gave him the pat response, "I'm sorry for your loss."

"Yeah, it never gets easy when you lose people. All the drug usage back in the day really wreaked havoc on his body later in life."

There was an awkward silence as they chewed some food and slurped their coffees.

Alice said, "So how do you do it? I mean, dead bodies, really?"

"I know it's weird, but I knew I wanted to be an embalmer since I was eight."

"No frickin way. Eight? That's crazy. How did you know?"

"I saw my grandfather in the casket. And there was just a strong fascination with the entire process. I watched him die over the months. He looked so frail, not anything like he was when he was alive. But when I saw him in the casket that morning, he seemed more alive and at peace than I had ever seen someone. It was at that very moment I wanted to take care of people after they died."

"Dude, that is some supernatural craziness right there."

"I don't know about supernatural, but I definitely felt something inside of me to pursue it."

"Yeah, I get it. I had that same feeling back in high school and knew I wanted to be a rockstar. That is definitely God, my friend. He set us up."

Freddy remained silent. He would normally argue his side, but this was Alice fucking Cooper he was sitting with, and he didn't want to disrupt what was going on here.

Alice read him like a book, "You don't believe in God, do ya?"

Freddy paused, then said, "Not really. No."

"I frickin knew it. Well, He believes in you."

At this point, Freddy felt a twinge of pain. He was biting his lip to be quiet. But he couldn't resist the invitation. "No disrespect," he said. "I just don't believe there's anyone out there other than us."

"Really, so we just came out of nothing and end up nothing?"

"Something like that. I've been around death long enough and seen no evidence of life after."

"Oh, man, I love this. So give me some perspective here. No church background? Religion? Nothing?"

"No church. Religion is a crutch for people to cope with loss. They need something to talk about. Something to anchor themselves to that which brings them peace."

Alice put down his plate of food and leaned in with an excited expression, "Oh, man, this is rich."

"I don't mean to offend—"

"Offend? No way. I hung out with Charles Manson. This is nothing, and yet it is something."

"What do you mean?"

"Come on. You have to realize there is something inside you that says there is something beyond us. It's there. You're just not letting yourself investigate."

Freddy set his plate down and leaned back in the chair. "I don't know, man. I don't want to argue."

"Oh, man, heck yeah, you need to argue, but just not with me. You need to argue with yourself. If you look deep within yourself man, like I mean really deep, then that's where you get to the core. That's where it's at, my friend."

Freddy didn't respond. He couldn't respond. The invisible walls within his mind repelled the bullshit of religion. The very same walls he had erected since the age of eight.

Alice continued, "Okay, come on, man. It's no joke to feel called to be an embalmer. You felt called, right?"

"Yeah, I guess so."

"Well, hot damn, that's what I'm talking about."

"What? I don't get it."

"You were called, Freddy. Who called you? That's the question you need to be asking. Who called you?" Alice was so excited. He had a fantastic grin that indicated he knew something Freddy didn't, and couldn't wait for him to find out what it was. It was like he knew what was inside the best-wrapped gift in the world, and his face was telling Freddy to open it. Freddy wasn't shocked about the turn of the conversation, but instead, by the stirring he began feeling inside. At first, he attributed it to the uncomfortable position of feeling like a peasant standing before a king. A rock legend king, that is. He couldn't explain his thoughts and internal feelings but chalked it up to the intimidating one-on-one convo with Alice Cooper.

"Are you a Christian?" Freddy asked.

Alice stood up and clapped his hands once. He said, "How did you know that?"

Freddy looked at him, puzzled.

He said, "I didn't tell you. Out of the thousands of other religions in the world, and you asked me that one? If you're asking me, then I know you didn't know before you met me. So who told you?" His eyes narrowed. "Freddy, who told you, seriously?"

"You are freaking me out a bit," he responded, "What do you mean who told me? It's just a guess."

He spun around while saying, "Come on, Freddy." He looked at him again with his dazzling blue eyes framed by his black hair. "I'm just challenging your thought process, is all. Don't get locked into trying to win a debate." He shook his head, "It's not about that. It's about you, the real you, your soul, that life-force inside of you finally hearing the truth, man."

"Your truth," Freddy corrected.

"No, man. All truths are not the same. It's up to us as humans to find the ultimate truth. The truth that trumps all truths."

"And where is this ultimate truth?"

Cooper pranced around the couch, slid back on to it, pointed his finger at Freddy, and said, "That's the start of a great adventure, my friend. Keep asking for the ultimate truth to show up."

Freddy took a deep breath and exhaled, "Mr. Cooper."

"Please, call me Alice."

"Alice. I don't like being labeled, but I'm an atheist. That *is* my ultimate truth. There's nothing out there."

Alice contemplated his next words. "Have you ever heard of C.S. Lewis?"

"Narnia?"

"Yeah, the Narnia guy. Did you know that he was an atheist?"

"Not really. Narnia isn't my style."

"What I'm trying to tell you, Freddy, is Mr. Lewis was an atheist, and then he wasn't. This guy's mom died when he was nine, and his father was a distant and demanding ass. Lewis decided there was no god at the age of fifteen. He basically grew up alone and saw nothing to indicate there was anything else out there. But as life went on, he found that he could make another decision, and things started to happen to turn him towards believing."

This story sank in while Freddy compared his own life to CS Lewis. His mother died when he was five, and his father was an alcoholic. He felt abandoned and raised himself.

Alice continued, "Now, this Narnia guy was smart. Real smart, like you. He didn't go into Christianity lightly. He questioned everything, but God wasn't afraid of his questions, and ultimately Lewis turned to him." Alice paused and then added, "I want you to pursue your questions instead of leaning on *your* crutch."

"What crutch is that?"

"Ignorance."

Ooo, that hurt. Freddy felt the jab, but Alice was right. He had his own crutch, ignoring the possibility that something else might be out there.

"I know that was harsh, dude, but I've been around for sixty-eight years and can read people pretty good. Some of us, like me, need a good kick in the ass. Just think about it, man—nothing happens by chance. This crazy world we live in—Science, our own bodies, which you know better than most, point to...something. Shouldn't we try to discover what that something is? Or conclude, perhaps, that something or someone is trying to get us to notice them, but we have blinders on? Just start paying attention as you go through life. He will give you signs. That's all I'm saying, man."

Freddy couldn't say anything. He was taking it all in. The internal security walls he had built since a child were on high alert. The questions that had defended his heart coming alive. Why didn't anyone save his daughter, Eve? Why hadn't any superpower deity save the other children killed by this maniac? Why was there evil in the world? Where was this loving God? All these questions, unanswered, and yet people still believed. Alice Cooper believed. He felt a breach in his wall. A slight crack.

Alice stood, "Hey, man, I hope I didn't overstep my boundaries with you. You seem like a really cool dude. Love the tats, man." He pointed to the exposed ink on Freddy's arms. "There's some good work done. What does that one mean?" His finger touched the white rose surrounded by thorny tendrils, like snakes, that were trying to choke it out.

Out of all my tats, he pointed to the one that meant the most to Freddy.

"The rose is my daughter, Evelyn."

Alice mumbled, "Man, that's beautiful. How old is she?"

"She died."

"Woah, dude, I'm so sorry to hear that. Was it cancer or something?"

For an unknown reason, Freddy responded. "The Angel Killer."

Alice instantly knew who he was talking about. His eyes widened in shock.

Freddy retreated, "I don't know why I even said that. I…"

"Wow," Alice's voice quieted, "I can't imagine."

Freddy took a deep breath and exhaled, "I should be going. Thank you for your time."

Alice said, "Hey, when I have a tour in San Diego let's hook up, okay?" He grabbed his cell phone on the glass table, "What's your number? I'll have my manager contact you with my schedule and we'll work something out. Listen, I don't do this kind of stuff with anyone."

Freddy mechanically rattled off his number and then Alice texted his manager his contact info with instructions.

"Thank you, Alice."

"You bet. Have a good flight home and don't forget about Narnia, okay?"

Freddy smirked in acknowledgment and shook his hand.

As he opened the door to let him out, he said, "Freddy."

He turned to face him, "Yeah."

"C.S. Lewis wasn't a Christian before he went to the zoo one day, but when he got there, he was. Don't over complicate things. Search for the truth. It's usually hiding in plain sight. God bless you, man. Hey, and I'm truly sorry to hear what happened to your daughter."

Freddy gave a half-smile and said, "Thank you. I appreciate your time and everything we talked about."

"My prayers are with you, Freddy. We'll stay connected for sure. I mean that."

Freddy turned and walked out. He heard the door click closed and his mind began to replay everything that had happened. Was this actually happening at all or was he about to open his eyes from a dream? No, it was real. This happened. He tried to wrap his head around the fact that he'd just had breakfast with Alice Cooper, but what dominated his mind the most was the story about the Narnia guy. It definitely got him wrestling. It got him thinking. It got him looking.

Details, subtle in nature at times, hit Freddy after his visit, the morning after, and all the way on their flight home. Something transpired within Freddy. Something he had never experienced before. It was spiritual, to the best of his limited knowledge, but profoundly moving. Before he left New York, he wasn't a believer in God. But when he landed in California, he was.

CHAPTER 10
NEW WINGS

T HE KEYS JANGLED with each step. Steven Murdock walked through the parking lot at Brengle Terrace Park in Vista. His eyeglasses were smudged as he pushed the bridge back on his nose. He scanned the area nonchalantly while picking up loose trash. It was an overcast night for fireworks, but still in the high sixties. Steven reflected on his instructions. God had told him it was time for another angel to be born. It was July 4th, 2016, three months after his last released angel. He worked for the Parks and Recreation Division for San Diego County. In his twenty-five years of service, he had tenured a unique position, overseeing the clean-up of all the North County parks. He worked on his own, had his own County vehicle, created his own work schedule, and had access to most park buildings. A County employee ghost, hidden within the system. He was an excellent employee but did not play well with others. County officials formed a special position in order to keep Steven. The specific words they said to him were, "We like you, Mr. Murdock, but we would like you to work alone. We have set up a new position for you." Now, he was out of sight and out of the minds of all bureaucrats.

Steven preferred to work alone. He understood that his god had arranged everything and called him for an assignment only he could perform. God told him this world wouldn't understand him. They labeled him the Angel Killer, but in reality, he was just the opposite; he was the Angel Deliverer. His god protected him. His god guided him. He heard his god's voice. Steven received dreams giving him instructions on how to kill the children quickly and without pain. His god was a merciful god. In Steven's eyes, it wasn't killing but instead releasing.

It was 8:31 pm. Fireworks would start at 9. There was a line of porta-potties just outside the north entrance to the amphitheater. This was the location god had instructed him to be at. A local cover band called The Mar Dels was singing just inside on the main stage. To him, it was dull background noise. Steven stopped to look at the baseball fields below him. Pyrotechnic specialists scrambled about, getting the final touches ready for the nation's big birthday celebration. The large amphitheater held thousands of people sitting in lawn chairs, built-in seats, or on blankets. Brengle Park was built on a hill surrounded by tennis and basketball courts, several baseball fields, frisbee golf, a playground, green grass, and trees. The amphitheater, situated at the top, was the crown jewel of the ninety-thousand residences calling Vista their home.

Steven checked his watch. 8:44 pm. He placed a partially full trash bag into the back of his truck, idling in the red zone area. Nobody paid attention to the County vehicle. It was twenty feet from the dozen porta-potties lined up along the decorative concrete wall guiding patrons to the amphitheater entrance. People were milling about, but most of them were getting situated for the big show. He checked his watch again. 8:52 pm.

He pulled out another trash bag, but this one was different. It was lined with a heavy material like a gunny sack with black plastic on the outside. It was Steven Murdock's method of transporting the children. Blending the bag in with other trash bags in the back of his truck bed, he pushed some tools around to make room. He checked his watch. 8:56 pm.

"It's time," he whispered. "Thank you, Lord, for the gift forthcoming."

Just then, a little girl raced ahead of her father. Her blonde pigtails bounced around as she held her crotch, "Daddy, hurry. I've got to go." Steven estimated her age to be five years.

The dad, in his business suit attire, was walking while looking at his cell. "I'm coming, baby. Go ahead and pick one of the bathrooms. I'll wait out here for you. Hurry, though, the show is going to start any minute. Okay?"

Steven made his way over. He checked his watch. 8:59 pm. Peripherally, he could see the dad paying attention to answering a message via text. His back was to Steven as he glanced up several times from his texting to observe the preparations in the field below.

The first firework shot up. It blared a bright red. All eyes were fixed on the single flare, and then it exploded, showering the sky with reds, whites, and blues. Cheers erupted. Choreographed music piped in through the speakers from KYXY 96.5FM. It echoed throughout the area as they cranked up the volume. Three more successive thuds fired from the ground, and three more brilliant showers lit up the sky.

The father was briefly mesmerized by the fireworks, then went back to his text.

Steven made his move, opened the porta-potty to find the little girl sitting down. She looked up with her beautiful big blue eyes, but Steven's face was shadowed by the streetlamp behind him. He quickly stepped in, grabbed her neck, and broke it. It sounded like someone cracking their knuckles. She went limp into his arms.

"Sweetie, you almost done?" the dad called.

Steven paid no attention to his voice and methodically pulled the gunny sack makeshift trash bag over her body, cinched it, and opened the door. The father was standing there dumbfounded, mouth agape.

Steven said, "I think your little girl is the next one over."

The man's face scrunched, "Oh, okay." He turned his attention to the next stall.

Steven followed quickly behind while letting the bag drop to the ground with a dull thud. The father opened the stall to find it empty but was shoved from behind. Steven had pulled out a knife and stabbed the man's back while pushing him in. The man lurched. Blood gushed out as Steven brought the blade to his throat and sliced him open. Steven pushed him, forcing the man to kneel down and have his head inside the toilet. The sound of blood hitting the feces-infested water below echoed, but it was quickly drowned out by the successive fireworks exploding overhead.

Steven stepped out of the stall, closed it, and looked around. No one was in the vicinity since everyone was watching the fireworks. He collected his trash bag, hustled to the truck, heaved it over the tailgate. Then he opened his door and escaped the area with no one any the wiser.

He made his way to Guajome Regional Park in Vista, less than seven miles away. It would be there he would deliver the next angel.

Steven could see the trash bag containing the girl in his rearview mirror. He said, "Don't worry, little one. You'll be getting your wings soon. Everything's going to be alright."

CHAPTER 11
JULY 4TH, 2016

"SHIT, EVEN I'M impressed," George stated as they entered the Moonlight Amphitheater at Brengle Terrace Park.

Freddy followed behind him, "Your first time here?"

"Yeah."

"I took Jenny here a couple times for some plays."

George scanned the area for someone, "How fucking romantic, dude." He turned to Freddy, "Now you have a romantic fucking date with *moi*." His perfectly straight white teeth gleamed.

"Screw you," Freddy laughed and pushed his face away.

George went back to scanning the area. Round tables were covered with white tablecloths topped with red and blue décor. They sat level on the top ledge of the semi-circle cascading theater, the focal point being the main stage. Thousands of people roamed the grounds. Some picnicked, while others were drinking and socializing in groups. The back hill had kids rolling down the grass, adults playing frisbee, a father throwing a nerf football to his son. Mothers grouped with their strollers and infants and ice chests seemed to be everywhere. It was a spectacular view, and everyone sported festive clothing to mark the July 4th celebration.

George whispered, "There you are, motherfucker." His voice strengthened, "Freddy, c'mon. Follow my lead."

George made his way along the wide concrete walkway at the top. They passed by the stairs leading up to the grassy hill area, then passed by the sound booth. Finally, they reached a guy dressed in full July 4th flag pants and shirt costume, holding a clipboard. He was looking down at the board when George startled him, "You owe me money, asshole."

The man, startled, had a painted flag on each of his cheeks and fireworks on his forehead while wearing a top hat that matched his outfit. He pressed his clipboard to his chest as he lurched backward. "Holy shit," the man said.

"Nothing holy about shit, Troy."

He regained himself, looking around in embarrassment, "George, what the fuck."

"Shhh, the children, dude."

Troy glanced around him to see if anyone was there. No one.

"I got you good, Troy. Just like old-times."

"Yeah, like whatever. What are you doing here?"

"Whataya mean what am I doing here? My friend and I are looking for a table."

Troy scanned his clipboard while biting his lower lip. He looked at George and then raised his left eyebrow while saying, "You're on my shit list, but you're not on *THE* list." He tapped his clipboard with emphasis.

George smiled, then said to Troy, "Check again. I think it's under Jass."

Troy smirked and then spotted the name, "Hugh?"

"Yeah, that's me. Hugh Jass."

Troy tilted his head, scoffed with a half-smile, and said, "Cute, for a fifth-grader."

"Ah, it was the best I could do on short notice. How are you doing?

"Doing alright. Looks like things are good for you."

"Troy, you know I got a job for you anytime you want it. Not sure why you want to keep getting abused by the city wearing ridiculous shit like this and helping people find their table."

"George, this isn't my job, and you know it."

"Yeah, well, whatever. Just know you can make some real money with me. It's hard to find people I can trust. You're a keeper."

"I appreciate that. I appreciate everything you have done for me and my family."

"I'm a giver," he glanced over at Freddy and smiled. "Where's our table?"

Troy pointed and said, "Enjoy. I gotta get these others checked in. I'll catch up with you later."

George walked past Troy and then swatted his ass, "Good game."

Troy yelped and then rolled his eyes. He quickly returned a smile to the next couple, waiting to be seated.

George sat at his table, which was set for six people. They were the first in their party to arrive. Freddy wasn't sure of the evening arrangement. All he knew was George needed a date and called him last minute for a fundraiser event. A waiter came over, "Drink order?"

George said, "Hell yes. What do ya got?"

"Sir, we have red, white, or beer."

George smirked, raised his eyebrows, "And?"

"Sir, those are the choices. No hard liquor. It's a family event."

Under his breath, "Fuck me."

Freddy chimed in, "We'll have a couple beers, thanks."

The waiter nodded and left.

"Dude," Freddy smacked George on the shoulder, "lighten up."

He sighed, "Yes, mom."

"So what's the deal with Troy over there? Did you guys hook up in a previous life or something?"

George scoffed, "Yeah. No, I dated his sister back in the day. High

57

school shit. My assistant set this show up for me and told me I needed to check in with Troy Burke."

The name suddenly dawned on Freddy, "Oh, shit, the Burke brothers?"

"Yep, the very same. Their sister Barbara didn't want anything to do with them."

"Wait, wasn't Troy's older brother kicked out of school or something?"

"Yeah, caught boning the hot sex-ed teacher in the bathroom."

"*That's* what happened to Mrs. Garcia? Holy shit."

The waiter dropped off their beers. It was 6:01 pm—a long way off until the fireworks show at 9.

Freddy changed the subject, "So what are we doing here again?"

George rolled his eyes, "Another fundraiser for the city. I gotta jostle my junk with the city mayor and her lackeys."

"No big deal. I'm just having dinner with the mayor," Freddy said.

"It's just Vista, dude."

"If it's just Vista, then why are we here?"

"Touché. I've got plans submitted at City Hall for another location. It's always good to be in good graces with those running the show. Just play it cool."

"Dude, I'm here for the food, drink, and the fireworks."

"Asshole. I knew I could count on you, my closest friend."

"I'm just here to keep you out of trouble."

George leaned back in his chair, clasped his hands behind his head, "Trouble? Whatever."

Freddy took a swig of his beer. George stared at him for a long moment.

"You staring at my beauty?" he mocked.

George bypassed the joke and said, "So what happened in New York? You've been different ever since we got off that plane like you had some type of near-death experience kind of shit."

Freddy set his drink down, wiped the foam from his lips, and stared back at George. Defiance came upon him. He couldn't explain it to George nor anyone else. "I don't know what the fuck you're talking about."

"See," George came closer, elbows on the table, "that's what I'm talking about. There's something rattling around in that noggin of yours. You always fucking do this. Hiding away inside your head."

"I'm not hiding. I'm right here."

George narrowed his eyes, grinned, "Yeah, right. Whatever, dude. You get fucking chatty with Alice and...I don't even know, cause you won't fucking tell me!"

Freddy noticed some parents looking over at them as their children were nearby, hearing George's colorful metaphors. "Listen, cool it. I'm fine."

"Bullshit."

The stage below them had teenage dancers from a local dance studio performing. The crowd applauded after each routine. It was 6:11 pm.

Two teenage boys approached, holding two-foot-long cardboard tubes with pictures of kids wearing glowing necklaces around necks and wrists. "We're raising money for the city to help the homeless. Do you want to buy any glow necklaces?" They weren't confident in their approach, eyes downward, and expected the following answer to be a no.

George said, "How much?"

They looked at each other with slight grins. "It's a dollar, sir."

"No, how much for all of it?"

Their eyes bulged in disbelief.

"Tell ya what," George took charge, "I'll give you each a $100, and then you pass out those lovely necklaces to all the kids. How does that sound?"

"Uhh, okay," one mumbled.

George pulled out his money clip and unsheathed two one-hundred-dollar bills. He handed them the money. "Okay, get going and hand those things out." They ran off as instructed. George and Freddy watched several of the kids in the area receive their unexpected gifts. Parents were unsure, but shrugged their shoulders as their children showed the colorful necklaces and bracelets that would be lighting up the area after dark.

George leaned in and whispered to Freddy, "I'm a fucking giverrr."

Freddy lifted his glass of beer, "Cheers to that."

The night went on. It was a BBQ feast. The menu included beef brisket, BBQ chicken, pulled pork, BBQ beans, macaroni salad, fresh green salad, and a smoked peach cobbler for dessert. George became the ultimate politician with the other guests who had eventually arrived at the table. Freddy did a lot of nodding and smiling but mainly watched the acts on stage.

The Mar Dels, a local cover band favorite, consisted of five men and two women. They started at 7:30 pm. He reminded himself that the fireworks were scheduled to start at 9. The Mar Dels were the final act for the evening. They played everything from Aretha to The Doors. The best part of the night for Freddy was watching all the children dancing in front of the stage, ranging in age from two to twelve. One little girl, about five, had the cutest pigtails. She was blonde with adorable blue eyes reminiscent of a character from a Disney movie. She wore a beautiful gold dress and loved to spin. Freddy caught himself smiling several times while watching her. He couldn't help but imagine she was his daughter dancing up there. He looked on like a proud father. A ghostlike image of his daughter Eve appeared, and both the girls grabbed hands and twirled to the music. Freddy caught himself laughing out loud from the pure joy of seeing his little girl having so much fun.

George noticed and tapped Freddy's shoulder, "Hey, you alright?"

Freddy regained his composure and said, "Yeah, fine." He looked back, and Eve was gone. Gone back into the dark recesses of his heart. A heart that he desperately wanted healed. But it was impossible without Eve in his life. He sort of understood the idea of having a god to focus on in hopes of seeing loved ones after this time we live in.

It was always proposed, *"What is after this life?"* His dad always told him "nothing." There was nothing out there but darkness. He told Freddy, *"Do you remember anything before you were born? It will be the same after you die."*

Now, though, with the tragic loss of Eve, he so desperately wanted to be united with her. Something happened on that plane ride home that was unexplainable. Freddy rationalized that, if he could emphatically state there was nothing after death without any proof, then he could also state that there *was* something after death without any proof. What did he have to lose?

9 pm. The first firework shot up. It blared a bright red. All eyes were fixed on the single flare, and then it exploded, showering the sky with red, white, and blue. Cheers erupted. The prearranged music, piped in through the speakers, echoed throughout the area.

Freddy nudged George, "Hey, I'm gonna take a leak."

"Now? You're gonna miss the show."

"After seeing all the kids today, I've seen the best show already. Thanks for bringing me along."

George smiled, "You bet, my friend. Need help holding that log of yours?"

Freddy rolled his eyes and said, "I'll be fine, thanks."

George chuckled. He watched his friend fade into the darkness. His silhouette coming into view from the light of the fireworks.

Freddy had been to the porta-potty area earlier in the day. He knew where he was going even though the park was fully dark to heighten the pyrotechnics. There was a long pathway up a steady grade leading to the upper parking lot area. The house lights had also been turned off to add more effect to the brilliant showers of fireworks exploding above. But a single streetlamp lit the way for safety reasons. A dozen blue, portable bathrooms stood at attention. The smell of a long day of battle against thousands of people wreaked havoc on the nose as he approached.

Freddy wouldn't miss the finale. He checked his cell. It was 9:08 pm. He opened the first stall and quickly closed the door. Vomit was everywhere. "Fuck," he said, placing his hand to cover his nose. He retreated to the next in line. He opened it to find a man in a business suit hunched over. Face deep in the toilet. He closed the door just as quickly as the first, "Sorry, dude. My bad."

Freddy cautiously opened the third one. It was clear, other than the smell. He stepped in. Fireworks continued to pound outside, and the music blared in sync. As he peed, he thought about the poor guy in the next stall over. How many times had he helped George in similar instances? Not tonight, however. He wanted to get back to the show. Freddy wasn't this guy's wingman. Someone else had to fill that job tonight because it wasn't going to be him.

One of the fireworks showered bright overhead, and a sparkle of glitter caught his attention inside the bathroom next to the toilet seat. He finished, zipped his pants, then inspected the glittery tassel. It was a gold ribbon. *"Some poor kid would be crying later to mom and dad about this,"* he thought. He remembered several meltdowns with his own daughter, Eve, about the smallest of incidents. Small to us but huge to our children. He left it there then went back to the show.

CHAPTER 12
THE MORNING AFTER

G EORGE HELPED FREDDY to the barstool at his kitchen counter. Freddy grabbed his coffee George had made him and he slowly brought it up for a sip. But then Freddy let the coffee topple out of his hands, stunned by what he saw on the T.V.

"Breaking news. Late last night, tragedy struck Brengle Terrace Park in Vista when patrons found a dead body inside one of the portable bathroom stalls. Hello, I'm Heather Myers, and welcome to Channel 8 Morning News. We start with a horrific scene as, last night, people leaving the celebration of our country's birthday on a high note found themselves in utter shock after two women discovered a middle-aged man dead and hunched over in the bathroom. It appears there was foul play. We go live to Steve Price, who has been on the scene throughout the night. Steve, what information do you have for our viewers?"

"Thank you, Heather. At 9:43 last night, two women found the now identified body of Christopher Choss, age 39, inside the porta-potty behind me. At first, they thought the man was sick. He was initially found with his head face down inside the toilet, but upon further inspection to find out if he was okay, they discovered the gruesome reality. The police were called, and the park has now become a crime scene. No information has been released on suspects or motives for this homicide. Heather, back to you."

"Steve, can you give us any details about what the two women saw and how they're doing?"

"Yes, they were pretty shaken, as you can imagine. They said there was quite a bit of blood coming from his neck. As they were trying to help the man, who they thought to be sick from alcohol consumption, they soon discovered he was, in fact, dead. We hope to have an interview with them later this morning."

"Wow, Steve. This is not a good start for everyone in San Diego on this Tuesday morning following the Fourth of July celebration."

George turned the T.V. off and perched himself in front of Freddy, "What the fuck happened?"

"I saw the guy. That guy," he pointed at the T.V. "I thought he was sick just like those women did. I thought about checking on him but didn't."

"Hey, dude, listen, it's not your fault. It must have been some drug deal gone bad or gang shit, who knows."

"Should I call the cops and let them know what I saw?"

George scrunched his face, "Cops? Dude, no. All you're going to do is just repeat the same shit the women told them. They got this. You just need to stay clear of it."

Freddy didn't respond.

"Dude, seriously, let it go. Now, if it was fucking me, on the other hand, who found the guy, then I would be freaking out. But you, you see dead people all the fucking time. Plus..."

"Plus, what?"

"Fuck, dude. Plus, you are pretty known in regards to you know who, and you don't want any more headaches with the media and shit."

"Yeah, I didn't think about that."

"That's why I'm here, good buddy," he grinned. George then pushed a new cup of coffee to Freddy and nodded for him to take it. Freddy grabbed hold of it and George coached the rim to his friend's lips. Freddy sipped. "There you go. That's it. Take in the sweet nectar of the gods." George lifted one hand and waved it in front of his face taking in the coffee's aroma and closing his eyes in ecstasy.

"Now, what do ya think? Good shit, huh? Those Columbians *must* be puttin' drugs in their coffee, my friend. Plain and simple."

Freddy stared at him, then took another sip.

"See, it's fucking addicting."

"George, it's called coffee. You know, caffeine?"

"No, this is the good shit. I have this stuff specially delivered. It is pure Columbian, bro. No artificial shit, no pesticides." While squinting, he brought all his fingers together, kissed them, and said. "Primo shit."

Freddy laughed, "I've got to go. I can't take any more of your bullshit."

George smiled, "Yeah, well, fuck off. I'm sending back your Christmas gift then."

"I thought you were a fucking giverrrrr," Freddy mocked.

George flipped him off.

"So we on for this Friday?" Freddy asked.

George rested his arms on the counter, "I don't know, dude."

"C'mon, you said you would."

"Indoor skydiving? It just sounds off. Sky...indoor. Get it? Why don't we do the real thing?"

Freddy stepped toward him, "Tell you what. Let's do this as a warm-up for the real deal."

"Seriously?"

"Yeah, why not?"

"Fuck yeah! I'll set it up."

"George."

"Yeah."

"Just make sure it's a legit fucking plane we're gonna jump out of."

He looked offended, standing up, placing his hand on his chest. "*Moi*? Legit is my middle fucking name, dude."

Freddy laughed as he walked away, heading out the front door. "Love you, bro."

George grabbed a small white towel and wiped the granite counter, "Love you, too, man."

George threw the towel over his shoulder and looked around his quiet palace, which overlooked the ocean from the Encinitas cliffs.

He took a deep breath, exhaled, and said to himself, "Well, now what? Crazy fucking world. I get to slice another deal while my friend goes off and slices up bodies."

He turned the T.V. back on.

It was the middle of the news broadcast. "New information has just come in. The deceased, Christopher Choss, apparently brought his five-year-old daughter to the park for the fireworks. She is now missing. With the Angel Killer on the loose, police are using all available resources to search for the five-year-old girl."

George exclaimed, "Fuck!"

CHAPTER 13
WHAT'S HAPPENING

Freddy's cell phone buzzed while he was driving. He snatched it from the drink holder. It was a text message from Jenny, WHAT'S HAPPENING?

He called her back. She answered. Her voice was soft, caring, but with a tinge of panic when she asked, "Freddy, are you okay?"

"Yeah, what's wrong? I'm driving to work."

"Just pull over."

Freddy was on the Pacific Coast Highway between Encinitas and Leucadia. He pulled over and parked in the dirt along the railroad tracks near two huge eucalyptus trees. "Okay, what's going on?"

"Freddy," she paused.

"What? Are you okay?"

"Yeah, I'm fine. It's just..."

"Just what, Jenny?"

"The Angel Killer."

Freddy's voice went lower, "What about him?"

"I guess he killed another girl last night. It's all over the news. They found her at Guajome Park."

He felt like the wind had been knocked out of him. He whispered, "What?"

"I wanted to call to see if you were okay. I know this—"

"Oh my god. This is fucking insane," Freddy said as he rested his forehead on the steering wheel. "Okay, so it happened last night? July 4th?"

"Yeah, apparently it's connected with someone killed at Brengle Terrace Park."

Freddy yelled, "Oh my fucking GOD!!!"

"What happened?"

"Jenny, I was at Brengle last night. I found the man in the fucking porta-potty but thought he was just puking. So, this guy had a daughter, and she was killed?"

"I think so. That's what they're saying."

"GOD would you FUCKING kill this guy, already!" He slammed his fist repeatedly into the center of the steering wheel, causing the horn to blare each time. "I can't take this anymore!"

Freddy heard Jenny's voice, "Freddy, Freddy, can you hear me?" He brought the cell back to his ear. "Freddy, are you there?"

He took a deep breath, exhaled, and answered, "I'm here." His voice was calmer.

"I'm here for you. I know this can set you off."

"Set me off? No, it's beyond setting me off, Jenny. This is two kids in three months. The sick fuck is probably jerking off somewhere and planning his next—"

"Stop it, Freddy. Just don't do that. Not with me."

"I'm sorry. Hey, listen. I've got to go. I'll talk later."

"Okay, I just...I just wanted to make sure you heard it from someone you know and not the news. George said—"

"Wait, George told you to call me?"

There was silence.

"Why the fuck did he have you call me?"

"I don't know. He said something like needing a female voice or something."

"Okay, I gotta go."

Freddy pressed the end button while Jenny was trying to say goodbye. The car was quiet. The Coaster train sped by him, kicking up dust and debris. He stared out his front window, unaffected by the sudden appearance of the train zipping by. He called George.

George answered, "Hey, bro—"

"Shut the fuck up!"

"Okay. Not talking."

"Why did you have Jenny call me?"

George didn't answer.

Freddy said, "Are you there?"

"Oh, did you want me to talk now? I was still on the first command of "shut the fuck up."

"Why? Why, Jenny?"

"Dude, I thought maybe a girl's voice would keep you calm and shit. I knew this would set you off again, and I didn't want you going batshit."

Freddy was calm, "George, don't do that again."

"Check, got it. Won't do it again. Hey, listen, where are you?"

"I've gotta go. We'll talk later."

"Okay, man, but—"

Freddy ended the call then leaned his head back. He closed his eyes and took another breath. The car motor hummed. He opened his eyes and looked at the car radio. He never listened to the radio. Sudden music ignited from the CD of a local band called Wasting June, but he hit the auxiliary button until it switched to the FM radio option. He didn't know what station to go to. The digital scanner stopped at a country station, so he tapped it again. This time it was rap. A third tap stopped at a station talking about the news, "...so having found the man to be the father of this little girl just exacerbates the emotions a hundredfold."

Freddy thought this newscaster sounded different. He sounded like he was talking in a normal voice and not a radio projected voice. He continued to listen.

"Can you imagine, not only losing your five-year-old daughter but also losing the father as well. This is a wake-up call for many of us. We need to understand that evil in this world is truly evil. Listeners, this brings the story of Jairus and his daughter to my mind. Let this story bring you hope while we emotionally wrestle with this horrible act that happened in San Diego, California."

Freddy was enraptured by the voice. He knew this wasn't a news channel but instead a talk-radio show of some kind. He wanted to hear the story.

The man continued, "So here you have Jairus in Mark 5. His daughter is dying, and he's desperate for a miracle. Listen to what it says. *'He begged Jesus, "Please come. My little daughter is dying. Place your hands on her to heal her. Then she will live." So Jesus went with him.'* Can you imagine this? His daughter is dying, and he has so much faith inside of him to approach Jesus and basically tell him what to do. Listen, you need to get this. This man told Jesus, the Son of God, what to do and what the result would be. Now *that* is faith. It is this type of faith, everyone, that has normal people like you and me raising others back from the dead."

Freddy's eyes widened. *"What did he say?"*

As if the radio speaker heard his thoughts, "You heard me, everyone, we can raise people from the dead if we have faith."

Freddy's mind was spinning. *"What is this faith he is talking about?"*

Again, as if the radio announcer was sitting next to him, "Now faith as we know it is confidence in what we hope for and assurance about what we do not see. It's all about confidence and assurance of not just what we believe but who we believe. This Jairus came to Jesus with confidence and faith. Now, check this out," the man continued. "A servant of Jairus' comes to him and says his daughter is dead. He goes on to say, don't bother Jesus to come and heal your daughter. Don't waste his time. Now, this next part is the crux of the story. Jesus responds. This is what The Bible says, '*But Jesus didn't listen to them. He told (Jairus) the synagogue ruler, "Don't be afraid. Just believe."*'"

Freddy thought, *"What happened next?"*

"Okay, so you're wondering what happens next. This is where Jairus has a decision to make. He could tell Jesus to not bother and thank him for his time, or he could believe in Jesus to do the impossible. Jesus was basically saying, "Hey, believe in me. I am going to bring your daughter back from the dead." Now, for us normal folk, that is a difficult pill to swallow, right?"

"Fuck, yeah, it is," Freddy answered aloud.

"Listeners, I pray you have ears to hear this story. What happens next is crazy. Jesus goes to Jairus' home, and there are tons of people in confusion and crying. There's no hope. Jesus comes in and basically tells everyone to get out. He wants all the confusion and hopelessness to leave. Jesus walks over to the girl, grabs her hand, and says, '*Little girl, I say to you, get up!*' And what happens? This girl gets up immediately and starts walking around. Isn't that amazing?"

Freddy responded under his breath, "Woah."

"Okay, so what do we do with this? God doesn't want believers just sitting around believing. He wants action. He wants our faith to ignite inside of us. God gave us a spirit of power, the kind of power to raise the dead. So let's get out there and raise those little girls in the world with the god-like faith that is within us."

Freddy turned the radio off and exhaled a breath he didn't know he was holding. He rested his head back and tried to relax. His thoughts were bouncing all around inside his mind until one thought rose above all other thoughts.

"I'm gonna fucking raise that little girl back from the dead."

CHAPTER 14
BODY SNATCHERS

IT WAS 7:54 am, July 5th, 2016. Freddy called his boss, Bob Knicker, as he drove to his office in Oceanside.

"Good morning, Freddy." Bob's voice had a congested nasal sound.

"Hey, listen, Bob, I need a favor."

"Sure, what's going on?"

"It's gonna be a doozy of a favor."

"Okaaayyy," he slowly drew the word out.

"I need you to arrange a pick up for me."

"Who's the decedent?"

"Location is Guajome Park."

"Are you talking about—"

"Yes."

"No bloody hell way, Freddy."

"Come on, Bob. You owe me."

"Yeah, I do, but this..." Bob took a deep breath and exhaled as he leaned back in his chair. "Okay, listen, I know someone at the Medical Examiner office. Let me give him a call."

"You da best. I'm on my way to pick up the chariot."

"Okay, see you in a few."

Freddy ended the call and sped up as he took the backroads to avoid traffic on the 5 Freeway leading up to the 78.

Now, Freddy felt like he had a purpose. He called his best friend.

George answered, "You miss me already?"

"I need a wingman."

George's voice changed. It sounded serious, "When and where?"

"I need you to fly like the wind. White button shirt, tie, and black pants. I'll text you the address to meet me."

"It's on like Donkey Kong."

BOB KNICKER WAS waiting outside the backdoor of the mortuary. The top of his head was bald surrounded by thin hair around the ears and back. His large gut and short body were accentuated by his white collared shirt and black tie. Freddy pulled up, parked his car, and got out.

"Bob, give me good news."

"Good news is I got an okay from Larry at the Medical Examiners. Bad news is you need to get there before Allen's team does."

"Shit! Allen? Those fucking idiots don't have a clue what they're doing."

Bob raised his hands in surrender. "I know, I know. You don't have to tell me."

"How the fuck did they even get the opportunity?"

"The owner knows a lot of people, so just like you are calling in a favor, so are they."

"How much time do I have?"

"Chariot is fueled. Keys in the ignition. You need to go now."

"Thanks, Bob." Freddy got into the white van and fired it up.

Bob mumbled under his breath as he waved goodbye, "I hope you know what you're doing."

FREDDY SPOTTED GEORGE in the Mission Plaza Real Shopping center off Mission Avenue in Oceanside. He pulled up next to him, standing by his orange and black mustang.

George's smile was so wide. "Fuckin A! This is happening!"

Freddy shook his head, chuckled, and said, "Today is your day, George." Freddy hopped onto the 76 Highway, which would take them to Guajome Lake Road.

"Okay, so what's the fucking plan?" George asked.

"Well, we drive to the crime scene, pick up the deceased, and…"

"Fuck me," George said. "Who are we picking up, and why do you need me?"

Freddy looked at George, "It's the Angel Killer."

"They got him?!"

"No, not him. It's the girl from last night."

"Fuck me, are you serious?"

Freddy didn't respond.

"Holy shit, man, I don't know about this."

"George, just relax and follow my lead. I'm not the best bullshitter, so that is where you come in. You will know if I need assistance. Just…"

"Just what?"

"Just…be you."

"Be me?" George turned pale. "Be me. Yeah, okay. I can do that."

He looked at Freddy and said, "I got you, bro."

"I know, my friend. Thank you."

George smacked Freddy's shoulder, "Fuckin A, dude. This is the shit."

"Okay, um, calm down a bit. I need you to be the *calm* you on this one."

"Yeah, no problem. You want calm. I can do fuckin calm. My middle name is calm."

"I thought it was—"

"Yeah, well, it's fucking calm today." George straightened his tie and focused his attention on the front of the van. His eyes were intense.

Freddy smirked as he turned right onto Guajome Lake Road. They were instantly met with a barricade of police cars. Media vans and trucks laced the side of the road on both sides. Film crews and newscasters were everywhere. Some innocent bystanders congregated behind the yellow tape line while two police officers enforced the blockade.

After flashing his credentials, another set of officers waved Freddy to proceed, lifting the yellow tape so they could drive under.

"Holy shit," George commented under his breath.

They took in the scene. Six police cars blocked the area while an ambulance, fire truck, and two black Crown Vics were also parked or idling in the park. Lights flashed in all directions from the vehicles. It was like every movie crime scene you had ever seen.

An officer further in waved them to drive to his location and park where he pointed. Two men wearing collared shirts and ties looked over to see the van approaching.

Freddy said, "George, those guys are homicide detectives. They are going to escort us to the body. You can't freak out, man. This is it."

George took a deep breath and exhaled. Then said, "I can do this."

Freddy put the vehicle into park and got out. He opened up the back and slid out the gurney. George assisted him.

The blue shirt man approached, "I'm Detective Barns. Can I see your ID?"

Freddy pulled out his license for body removals and handed it over. George continued to fiddle with the gurney.

Detective Barns said, "You're with Pinewood? I thought Allen's was coming to retrieve."

Freddy smiled, "Larry at Examiners Office made a last-minute change. We had the best position to respond since we're located in Oceanside."

Barns handed Freddy's ID back with a measured stare that caused Freddy to look away.

Freddy said, "We all good?"

"Yeah," Barns said, "We're good." He held the stare on Freddy for another second before turning his attention to George. "You look familiar to me," Barns said, He narrowed his eyes, trying to recollect where he had seen George from. "ID?"

Freddy quickly said, "He's in training, and his ID hasn't come in yet."

George jumped in, "Yeah, I'm the newbie," then gave a cheesy smile.

"I'd pack up that smile, George. Not a very cheerful moment we're in."

George's lips pursed, "Yeah, check, no smile." His pointer and thumb came together, and he made the zip-it-up gesture.

"This way, guys. Please make sure to avoid any of our markers as this is an active crime scene. No talking to anyone. You are to retrieve the body and deliver it directly to the Chief Medical Examiner, Dr. Glenn Wagner. He is waiting for your arrival. Do you both understand?"

"Yes," both of them said in unison.

George pushed the gurney while Freddy guided it from the front. They followed Detective Barns down a narrow path. The path ended at a small clearing along the lake. The water lightly lapped up onto the shore. There was a rich smell of duck shit and vegetation. Yellow cones with numbers were strewn all around them, marking possible clues that could lead them to the Angel Killer's identity.

George gasped as the body was displayed openly in the clearing. A naked little girl, age 5, blonde hair with pigtails. The skin from her back was fanned out from either shoulder instantly bringing the imagery of wings sprouting from the child's back.

"Maybe your newbie should wait at the car," Detective Barns said. "I don't want him throwing up on my crime scene."

Freddy looked at George, "You're good, right? You've got this."

George looked at him. He could tell it was close, but he recovered. "I'm good. Really, I'm fine."

"Okay," Freddy said, "get the bag out, unfold it, and lay it next to the body."

"Roger that."

Freddy turned to the detective, "I hope you catch this mother fucker once and for all."

Detective Barns wasn't ready for the comment at first, "Yeah, I've been on this case for ten years. My partner, thirteen. Whoever it is will mess up eventually. We hope we get something this time."

Freddy stared at the little girl as George apprehensively approached with the body bag.

Detective Barns said, "Hey, I know this hits home right now."

Freddy looked at him. "You know who I am?"

"Yes, Freddy, I do. I know all the parents who have suffered. Hell, I fear for my children as well."

"Why'd you let me in?"

He looked at Freddy hard, "I don't know, to tell you the truth. I shouldn't have, but something told me you needed to do this."

"Something?"

"C'mon now, this ain't no voodoo bullshit." His eyes narrowed, "I knew you would take care of her as your own." They both looked at the body.

Just then, the other detective showed up, "Barns, looks like we have another pick-up team that arrived. What's the word?"

Barns looked at Freddy. Freddy quickly said, "Hey guys, I mean detectives, there was a mix-up. Allen's should have been called off. I'll have George go and talk to them."

The detectives looked at each other. Then the other said, "Okay, follow me."

Freddy looked at George and winked.

Freddy proceeded to get the transport bag ready. He fought the fact that he was picking up a little girl he had watched just hours earlier dancing. Every child lost by the hands of this killer was like his own child being killed, all over again. Instead of sorrow and depression, it was rage and revenge that filled his heart.

"I will embalm the motherfucker alive," he said under his breath.

"What was that?" Barns asked.

"Nothing, just a prayer, detective."

"Yeah, I've been praying too. We need all the prayers we can get to find this asshole."

Freddy was able to lift the little girl on his own and lay her into the bag. He zipped it up, looking at the girl's faded eyes. She wasn't there any longer. The body was an empty shell. He brought the bag to the gurney.

He could hear George talking as he rolled up the pathway and out into the parking area.

"I don't care about what your little piece of fucking paper says on it. We were given strict orders from the Examiner."

"And what is his name? You seem to be forgetting that part," the red-head freckled face man said.

"Look, maybe if you guys were competent like Pinewood, then you would be getting exclusive pick-ups like we do. Hey guys, don't let this be a jealousy thing. It's a win for both sides."

"A win? How do you see it as a win?"

Freddy came into view. "Oh, look, boys. Here comes the win now," George pointed with a smile. George instantly dropped the smile when he saw the detective looking at him. "My bad."

George said, "So, Dick, let's just—"

"It's Will, asshole."

"Will, Dick, same thing. So, let's just have you get out of our fucking way so we can bring this little girl home to Papa at the Examiner... place, whatever."

"Hey, Will," Freddy acknowledged his competition.

"Freddy."

Freddy shrugged as he loaded the gurney into the van. "What can I say, Will? Better luck next time."

"Fuck off!" Will tapped his partner and said, "C'mon, let's go."

George got into the van. Freddy closed up the back then got into the driver's seat. They now had the Angel Killer's latest victim.

"What a bunch of pricks," George said.

Freddy drove past the barricade and onto the highway.

George said, "Now what?"

Freddy looked at him, "Now, we're gonna do something crazier than anything you have ever done before."

George's face scrunched, "Crazier than body snatching a dead girl?" He saw the glint in Freddy's eye. "Dude, my life is so boring without you. Marry me."

CHAPTER 15
DEAD RAISING 101

"IF YOU TAKE me back to my car, I'm going to beat the living shit out of you," George pointed his finger at Freddy.

Freddy looked at him for a long moment. "Fine, but this is going to be crazy. I mean really fucking crazy."

George smiled, and his eyes became super intense, "Crazy is my middle fucking name, dude. Now drive."

Freddy drove South on the 15 Freeway toward the Medical Examiner Office in Kearny Mesa.

George was quiet for a little while but eventually asked, "We're not taking her to the Examiner place, are we?"

"Nope."

"I shouldn't ask, right?"

Freddy didn't respond.

George couldn't resist, "Okay, what the fuck are we doing? What's the game plan?"

Freddy sighed, then said, "If what I'm about to do works, then we won't need to take her to the Medical Examiner Office."

"Freddy, what the fuck are you talking about? I'm gonna need more than that."

"I warned you it's crazy. We are almost there." He exited Ted Williams Parkway. Five minutes later, he pulled into a construction site and drove around the back of a partially built medical facility. He backed up into a delivery truck bay, parked, and shut off the engine. Freddy got out. George followed.

"Where the fuck are we?" George asked.

"An old medical building held up with legal issues. It's been on hold for the last year."

"And why are we here?" He swung his arms around as he spun.

Freddy opened up the back door to the van. "George, what I'm about to do has no words for me to tell you. I just hope it works." He slid the gurney and pulled the wheels to full extension. The white bag containing the five-year-old rested in front of them.

Freddy began to unzip the bag, then stopped, turned to George, and said, "I need you to trust me. I have to do this. And I'm thankful you are here with me."

George looked visibly nervous but nodded his approval. Freddy continued to unzip the bag and then pulled it away. The unnamed girl was pale, motionless, staring off into space. George was able to contain the contents in his stomach the first time but not now. He threw up. Freddy kept his eyes on her. A ghostlike image of his daughter, Eve, materialized and sat up to look at him. "Daddy, help me." The voice was hollow and distant.

Freddy said, "I'm here, baby."

George started coughing and spitting against the concrete wall of the sunken delivery bay.

The ghost reached out toward Freddy. "Daddy, help me."

Freddy's eyes glassed over, "Oh, baby, I'm right here. I'm gonna bring you back."

George sputtered again but turned, "What did you say?"

Freddy ignored George, or perhaps he didn't hear him. His focus was on the vision of his daughter, Eve, pleading for help.

With tears streaming down his cheeks, Freddy said, "I'm sorry, baby. I wasn't there to protect you, but I'm here now."

George said under his breath, "What the fuck?" The dead little girl was motionless with her skin falling off her shoulders, revealing dark meat and yellow fat. George could feel more bile coming up. He covered his mouth while gagging.

Freddy was in a trance, locked onto his daughter within his mind. He slowly reached out to touch her, but his hand was floating in empty space above the corpse. His eyes were focused on his ghost-daughter, sitting up looking at him.

"Help me, daddy. I need you."

"Oh, baby, I'm not going anywhere. I'm here to get you back and bring you home to mommy and me." More tears streamed down his face.

George regained his composure and reached out to his friend, "Freddy. Hey. It's me." He watched his friend gripped in some strange trance, and his arm extended as if reaching for someone that wasn't there. "Freddy!"

Freddy suddenly snapped out of it. The image of Eve vanished as she cried out, "Don't leave me!"

He lunged for her, "No!"

George grabbed hold of him and turned him, so they faced each other. "Freddy, it's alright, man. I'm here."

He crumpled into his arms, "George, I lost her."

"I know, man. She's gone. Let it out. I'm here."

Freddy wailed the cry he had held in for years. All the pain of losing his daughter and then losing his wife. George kept his friend lifted up as he felt his body go limp in exhaustion. "Dude, I've got you. I'm here." He spoke over him soothingly.

Minutes elapsed. Freddy stopped wailing, but tears and snot continued to fall. George held him up. He wasn't going to let his friend down. He had waited a long time for this and knew it would come.

Freddy eventually pulled away, head down, wiping his nose and eyes with his hand and sleeve.

George bent lower to connect with Freddy looking down, "Dude, it's okay."

Freddy slowly looked up. Still sniffling and eyes glassy, "George, I have faith."

"Of course," he responded while grabbing each of his shoulders. "You have incredible faith, man."

"I have faith," Freddy repeated.

George nodded but became nervous because of his friend's tone.

Freddy turned his head to look at the little girl. "I have faith."

George now turned from agreement to confusion. Something was wrong. Freddy returned to his trancelike state, repeating he had faith.

George said, "Freddy, come on. Stay with me."

Freddy grabbed hold of the little girl's cold hand.

"Stay with me, Freddy."

Freddy mechanically said, "Little girl, I say to you, get up."

George was stunned and froze. Two seconds elapsed. Nothing happened.

Freddy repeated it again, but with more emphasis, "Little girl, I say to you, get up."

Nothing happened.

"Little girl, get up!"

George tried to redirect Freddy, but he pulled away violently. "GET UP!"

George had his hands extended out, frozen in place, looking at his friend and then to the corpse. Nothing happened.

Freddy slowly turned toward him, "She's supposed to get up, George."

Freddy's knees buckled. George caught him and lowered him to the ground. "Okay, okay. It's alright."

Freddy mumbled, "She was supposed to get up."

"I know, I know. It's alright. Shhhhhh."

"Why didn't she get up?"

George cradled him, "I don't know, my friend. I don't know."

Several minutes passed. George broke the silence, "Yeah, next time you say we're gonna do something crazy, I'm gonna believe you. That was fucking crazy."

CHAPTER 16
ONE MONTH LATER

I t was Friday morning, August 5th. A month had passed since the failed dead raising incident when Freddy stepped into the reception office where he was greeted by his best friend, George. With a consoling voice, "Hey, buddy. How ya doing?"

Freddy smiled and nodded, "Good. A little nervous."

"Ah, nothing to be nervous about. This shrink is amazing, plus she's hot."

Freddy smirked, then there was an awkward silence.

George quickly said, "Hey, let's get you checked in." He guided Freddy to the receptionist.

"Good morning," the dark-haired woman said in a peppy voice. She wore black-framed glasses and a frilly white short-sleeved blouse.

"Hello."

"First time?"

"Yes."

George leaned over and added, "Be gentle with him."

"What's your last name?" She ignored George.

"Um, Foley."

"Please fill out the attached information. Dr. Beckman will be with you shortly."

Freddy took the clipboard and then sat with George. He began filling it out.

George spoke softly, "Dude, I've been seeing Dana for years. Look how good I've turned out. You're gonna be fine."

Freddy peered over at him with a skeptical look.

George relented, "Okay, maybe I'm not all the way put together, but it could've been way worse if I didn't see her. Trust me. This is gonna be good for you."

Freddy went back to filling out the paperwork.

Fifteen minutes had passed. Freddy turned in the clipboard. George was on the phone, talking loud while trying to keep his curse words hushed.

"Frederick Foley," the receptionist called, "Dr. Beckman will see you now."

Freddy got up and began to walk timidly toward the fogged glass door with the doctor's name on it in solid white block letters.

George got his attention with a loud whisper, covering the mic on his cell, "Hey, buddy, you got this. I'll be here when you're done." Freddy wasn't sure why George was here, but he was glad he was.

Dr. Beckman's office was pristine. Two cream-colored chairs were in the corner next to the window. They were angled toward each other but not full facing. They were each decorated with pillows and comfy looking blankets. In between was a glass tabletop with four wooden legs. A bowl filled with colored beads sat on top. Dr. Beckman sat behind a large mahogany executive desk with a matching bookshelf behind it on the opposite side of the room.

She stood and greeted Freddy, "Good morning, Mr. Foley. Please come in." She came around to shake his hand and gestured to the chairs in the corner.

"I was expecting a couch or something," Freddy mused.

She chuckled. "We've evolved over the years. Come and sit."

Dr. Beckman was tall and slim. She wore a tight black skirt that went below her knees and accentuated all her natural curves. She topped it with a champagne silk blouse. He could barely see the outline of her white bra underneath, not that he was looking. Freddy sat down while she went to a side cart with a pitcher of water and two crystal glasses. She poured water into each and turned around in time to see Freddy staring at her rear-end.

"Water?" she smirked.

"Yes, please. Thank you." He grabbed the glass from her and took a nervous sip. Her complexion was perfect. She had high cheekbones, and the slight slant of her eyes suggested Asian descent. Black hair draped over her shoulders. There was a hint of auburn weaved in as the light from outside caught it within the curls.

"So, Mr. Foley, what brings you in today?"

"You can call me Freddy."

"Perfect. You can call me Dana. So tell me about yourself."

Freddy placed his glass down and leaned back a bit. "Well, I'm an embalmer. Been doing that for over twelve years. I graduated top of my class at National University of San Diego in La Jolla. Got married in 2009, divorced 2014. Shouldn't you be writing any of this down or something?"

"Freddy, I know a little bit about you, and I know this is your first time visiting. I will use a term the outside world uses, your first time visiting a 'shrink'. I'm sure you've heard all kinds of things about what we do. Maybe you believe I can read your mind or psycho-analyze you and deem you bonafide crazy. All of that is not true. What is true is I am here to help you walk through the darkness in your life and bring some light into the picture so you can see things more clearly. Everything you tell me is strictly confidential and not shared with anyone. Does that make sense?"

"Yeah."

"Your friend, George Casey, speaks very highly of you. I have not taken a new client for quite some time. It's because of him that we are here today talking. I said I would sit down and give you a session and, after this session, I would make the decision as to whether or not to continue. So, with that said, I want to be crystal clear with you, Freddy, how we move forward from here is, respectfully, in your court."

"I understand."

"Okay, good. Now that we have all the chit-chat done, let's begin. Tell me what's really going on. Tell me the deep questions that you want answered. Tell me your hurts, your pains, and what you want to see dealt with in your life."

Freddy grabbed his glass and took another sip of water. He wasn't sure where to begin. He wasn't totally convinced she wouldn't lock him up in some psych ward if he revealed his intent to raise a girl back from the dead. He thought it best to steer clear of that.

"Um, I lost my daughter two years ago."

"I'm sorry to hear that. What is her name?"

"Evelyn. We called her Eve."

"That's a beautiful name. How old was she?"

"Five."

"Tell me about Eve. I want to know her."

Freddy took a deep breath and began to settle in, "Well, she was, I mean is, incredible." His voice grew stronger with pride. "Eve always had the cutest giggle. I think she got it from her mom. It would make anyone laugh. I would make the sound of an elephant, and that would get her going every time. I would do it in the grocery store when she was sitting in the cart, and people would come around from other aisles just to see who was giggling."

"That is so precious. What an angel," Dr. Beckman said. She watched Freddy clam up after her statement. She knew something was wrong.

"What's wrong, Freddy? What did I say that caused your mood to shift right now?"

"Nothing. I'm fine."

"This is where you have an opportunity to expose more of the darkness I was talking about. You need to trust me, Freddy."

"How? How can I trust you or anyone else? Nobody knows what I've gone through."

"This is true. Tell me what you're going through."

Freddy continued to tense up.

"It's okay, Freddy. I'm not writing anything down. I'm just someone listening to you. Isn't that what you want? Someone to listen to you?"

"I don't know what I want."

"Yes, you do. I think you know exactly what you want, and you're afraid to say it."

Freddy stared at the silver cart against the wall. The pitcher of water on top of it. The silver was scratched and reminded him of his embalming table at work. It suddenly calmed him as he focused on it. His breathing settled.

Not looking away from the cart, he said quietly, "I want my little girl."

Dana didn't respond but continued to stare at him. A long moment passed.

"I want my little girl back," he stated again. His eyes now connected with the psychologist. They stared at one another for what seemed like an eternity.

Dr. Beckman said casually, "Bullshit."

Freddy blinked, "What?" He was confused by her response.

"Bullshit. What do you really want, Freddy?"

"I just said I want my daughter back. What else is there?"

She took a deep breath herself, exhaled, but maintained her solid locked gaze on him. She was waiting for Freddy to say something else.

"What do you want from me?" his voice exploded.

"I want the truth. And I want you to hear it."

"What the fuck are you talking about? What truth? The truth that...that, I'm fucking upset. That this world doesn't fucking make sense. That I fucking hate you and your prissy little office. That my wife left me because our fucking daughter was butchered by some fucking crazy maniac that no one can find. That, that, I don't know, that I fucking hate myself and everyone that looks at me thinks 'there goes that guy that let his daughter get killed'." Freddy stood and yelled, "FUUUUCCCKKK!"

BACK OUT IN the reception area, George looked at the receptionist as they heard Freddy yell and said, "He's alright. It's fine, I'm sure. Sounds like it's going good in there."

She went back to typing on her laptop.

George stood from his seat and approached her, "Hey, listen. I'm having a few friends come over to a party Saturday. I was wondering—"

"I'm busy," she cut him off.

He tapped the counter with the palm of his hand, "Yeah, of course. It was last minute." He backed away, "Maybe next time."

DR. BECKMAN SAID, "Keep going, Freddy. You're standing at a door right now. It's a door you're afraid to open. I'm here with you. Don't be afraid."

Freddy sat down, put his hands to his face, "I just can't."

"Yes, you can. Let me guide you. Close your eyes."

Freddy looked at her.

"Close your eyes, Freddy. Trust me."

He slowly closed them.

"Now, I want you to relax and envision a door in front of you. Do you see the door?"

"No, it's dark."

"That's okay. You're doing great. Just relax. I want you to take a deep breath and let it out slowly."

Freddy inhaled and exhaled. His eyes fluttered open.

"Keep your eyes closed, and now sit back with your arms on the chair."

He did as instructed.

"Take another breath and let it out slowly. You're doing great, Freddy."

He followed her lead.

"You're in a safe place, Freddy. Just listen to the sound of my voice." She paused for a second. "Concentrate on the door that is coming to your mind right now. Do you see it?"

"Yes."

"Describe it."

"It's uh, wood, but old and has like splintered areas all over it. It's dark. It doesn't have a knob but instead the handle is a latch that has rust on it."

"Okay, good. That is great. Now reach out and open it."

Freddy slowly lifted his hand and reached for a make-believe door in her office. Dana watched him as she encouraged him further. She wasn't surprised by Freddy's physical reaction. "Good, now open the door, Freddy."

Freddy could see the dark and mysterious door. His hand was on the latch. He pressed the thumb latch down, and heard the door click open. He pulled, and light poured out from behind it. The light blinded him for a second, but then he saw a figure beyond. "I see something," he said aloud.

"What do you see, Freddy?"

"It's...it's a person, I think."

"What are they doing?"

"I can't see. It's too bright."

"Freddy, I want you to step into the light."

"I can't. I'm afraid. I don't know what's in there."

"I know. It's gonna be okay. I'm here with you. You are not alone. Just take a short step inside."

Freddy was scared, "But who is it in there?"

"I don't know, Freddy. Let's find out. Did you take a step in?"

Freddy's breathing increased.

Dana calmed him, "It's alright. Slow your breathing. I'm here with you."

"I did it. I took a step."

"Good, Freddy. Keep going until you can see what's in there."

He took another step. "I see someone. They're kneeling. I can't see the face."

"That's good, Freddy. Keep going. Tell me what you see."

He took another step. "It's a man. He's...working...or digging. His back is to me."

"Keep going, Freddy. Find out what he is doing."

He took another step. He was now looking over the man's shoulder and saw his daughter. She was dead. The man was pulling her skin out to form wings. "It's HIM!"

"Who is it?"

"It's the Angel Killer. He killed my daughter. I can see her."

Dana looked concerned. Freddy still had his eyes closed. His face was scrunched in disgust. "Freddy, I want to know what you really want right now. What is it you really want, Freddy?"

Freddy continued to watch the amorphous figure of a man prepping his daughter for the media to find. The man who brought his entire world crashing down. The man that destroyed everything he cared about.

"I want...justice." Freddy began to weep. "I want justice." His voice cracked. "I just want justice for my little girl."

Dana cautiously continued, "What is the root of this justice you seek, Freddy?"

Freddy's tears stopped flowing. He wiped his nose with his sleeve. "I want justice."

"Justice is the tree. What is at the root of the tree, Freddy?"

He sniffled. He took a deep breath that quivered and let it out. The answer came from deep within him. It was the source of everything that drove him forward. "Revenge."

Freddy opened his eyes and looked right at Dr. Beckman. There was a passion in his voice. A determination. A resolve. An answer. "I want to embalm this mother fucker alive!"

CHAPTER 17
DOGGIE STYLE

"So SHE TOLD you to walk into the light? That's some Poltergeist kind of shit, dude," George said. He took another bite of his In-N-Out Double-Double burger.

Freddy stared out the side window of his car. It was dark outside. Streetlamps revealed a park on the opposite side of the street. Freddy stared at the dimly lit pathway that zig-zagged amid the grass, off and out of sight. He could see a parking lot in the distance.

George crammed several fries into his mouth while saying, "Why this fucking park, dude?"

Freddy didn't look at him, "I don't know. Why not?"

George shrugged as he chewed, "You gonna eat those?" He indicated the loose fries at the bottom of the bag.

Freddy glanced and said, "Go for it." He checked his cell. It was 11:51 pm. Two weeks had passed since his first meeting with Dr. Beckman. She unleashed something inside of him. He had to do something. He mapped out all of the parks in San Diego County but realized the area was too vast. Narrowing it down to North County, he decided to choose Sunset Park in San Marcos. For the last four nights, he and George had come to this same location and watched into the early morning hours. He knew it was a Hail Mary, but he had to roll the dice. There were hundreds of parks and no telling when or where the Angel Killer would strike again. It was sometimes years before another victim showed up.

"Hey," George nudged him, "did you know about this?"

Freddy looked. George pointed to something at the bottom of his cup, holding it up into the light from outside. It said 'John 3:16'. "What is it?" Freddy looked confused.

"It's fucking from the Bible, dude."

Freddy's face registered unbelief, "How do you know that's from the Bible?"

"Another friend of mine told me. Isn't that fucking crazy?" He chewed on a fry and smiled.

Freddy went back to looking out the window.

George said, "Do you know they have some secret menu and shit there?"

"What, like the animal style?"

"Yeah, but did you know they have other shit?"

"Like what?"

"Ah, there is the 4x4, cheese fries, oh, and they have a killer grilled cheese sandwich. Their cheese is fucking amazing."

"I'll have to try that sometime."

George started giggling.

"What?"

"Nothing, just remembered I fucked with a friend of mine about ordering something secret on the menu that didn't exist."

Freddy smirked, "What happened?"

"Okay, well, I got the idea from someone else who told me to order my burger *Monkey Style*."

"What's that?"

"Supposedly, it's animal style burger, but they add in fries. Totally fucking bogus. I was placing my order at the drive-thru and ordered my burger, *Monkey style*. The lady tried to correct me to Animal, and

I said, "No, Monkey." We went back and forth until I finally said just add some fries to the animal style. She said they couldn't do that. So anyway, I went back and told him what happened, and he started busting up laughing. Yeah, fucking good one, dude."

Freddy chuckled.

George continued, "So it got me thinking, and I pulled the same thing on another friend of mine, but this time I convinced him to say, 'Doggie Style'."

"No, shit. Did he do it?"

"Yeah, so he thought I was fucking with him, but I told him that only employees know about this, so no regular people do this. I told him he had to give his employee number first. I got someone's real number and gave it to him. So he fucking goes up to the cashier, dude, not even the fucking drive thru. This gets rich."

"No fucking way, the cashier, inside?"

"Yeah, so he strolls up and gives them his employee number. She punches it in and says okay, what's your order. He then says proudly he wants his burger Doggie Style. A mother and her kids were standing off to the side and heard him. She fucking pulls the kids away and gives him that dirty mom stay away from my children look. I was fucking dying when he told me what happened."

Freddy laughed, "That is fucking awesome."

"Yeah, that was good."

Freddy said, "So how many friends of yours have you fucked with?"

He shrugged, "All of them." Then George smiled, showing his big gleaming white teeth. "But my best friends are the ones I tell about all the people I fucked with. That's the difference, and don't you fucking forget it."

"Dude, whatever. You have given me so much shit over the—"

George stopped suddenly, staring past Freddy, "What's that?"

"Don't fuck with me, George." Freddy slowly turned to look out the window. Then he also saw it. It was someone carrying something over his shoulder as they walked down the concrete pathway. They both watched, mouths open, as the individual walked out of sight into the darkness.

The inside light came on as Freddy opened his door.

George said, "Holy shit. It's on, dude."

They crept across the street, cut through the damp grass, and made their way to the concrete path. It was now after midnight, and the park was deadly silent. George carried a crowbar. Freddy had his cell phone ready to record. The plan was to record anything, maybe knock the killer out, and call the police. Freddy envisioned having the Angel Killer loaded into his trunk, taken back to his work, and embalming him live. He knew that wasn't possible. But it didn't stop him from dreaming.

They both heard noises further down. There was a clump of trees and bushes between them and the sand volleyball court. The sounds came from the bushes. They heard what sounded like dirt and leaves being pushed away, and grunts and moans, like someone was in pain.

Freddy started his recording and nodded to George to go first with his weapon. George was solid as a statue. His muscles bulged through his t-shirt as he gripped the crowbar. Adrenaline coursed through his veins. There were no other thoughts. They were on autopilot. The only mission was to hurt whoever was within these bushes. Freddy imagined them finding the Angel Killer but at the same time finding another child at his feet. He pushed the thoughts aside and could only imagine saving future children from the torture and horror that awaited them if they didn't do anything.

The leaves were thick, and George tried to walk stealthily, but each step crunched underfoot. His steps, however, didn't stop the struggling just a little further in. Whatever sounds the Angel Killer was making was masking their footsteps. George looked back at Freddy and indicated with a nod that they were feet away. Freddy felt droplets of sweat dripping down the back of his neck. This was it. This was his moment. He nodded to George to go for it. He nodded back. They held their breaths. George charged.

"Mother fucker!" he yelled.

Freddy was right behind him with the video going. George pulled his arms back, ready to swing at the silhouetted person who was on his knees. There was someone in front of him. Most likely, a child. The Angel Killers next victim. George held back his swing as they scared the shit out of the assailant, and he fell away to the side with his hands up in the air.

George and Freddy instantly saw the ass of a woman and her lover on his side with his pants down. Both of them froze as their minds tried to process the instantaneous transformation from the Angel Killer working on his next victim to the guy getting it on with his girl in the bushes of a park.

The guy grabbed his shoulder, scrunching his face in pain. "What the fuck?" he gasped. The woman began scooting away, frantically tugging her dress down while screaming at the top of her lungs.

George held up his hands, one was still holding a crowbar, and said, "Hey, woah, woah, hold on. We're so sorry. Um." He began to back away.

Freddy, dumbfounded, still recording, snapped out of his trance. He backed away. He and George took off like bats out of hell toward the car. They jumped in and peeled off as fast as they could.

George put his head back against the headrest, "What the fuck was that?"

Freddy faltered, "I thought for sure...it...it was him."

"No shit. That was crazy, dude."

They sped off down La Mirada, away from the park.

George suddenly began to crack up. It slowly built into a hysterical fit of contagious laughter. Freddy had to pull over to the side. They both were holding their stomachs and snapping their heads back and forth in hysterics.

As George was laughing, he said, "Doggie-style!"

CHAPTER 18
I'M YOUR BOYFRIEND NOW

"**D**UDE, THIS MOVIE seriously sucks ass," George said as he drank his beer.

Freddy had a bowl of popcorn in his lap and, without thought, chucked a kernel in his mouth as they watched A Nightmare on Elm Street. "Shhh, this is my favorite part."

"Really?"

The music from the TV grew louder as the scene unfolded. The main character, Nancy, just pulled the phone cord from the wall and placed it on her bed. She went to her bedroom door and peered out into the hallway.

"Dun, dun, dunnnn," George played the invisible piano, "Of course the fucking telephone is going to ring."

Freddy said, "Yeah, dude, the best fucking line of the movie is coming. I can't believe you haven't seen this."

Nancy slowly walked back to the bed, the theatrical music was loud, she grabbed the cord to inspect it, then answered the phone. "Hello?" she said.

"Here it is," Freddy whispers.

George was frozen, waiting for the one-liner.

The villain said on the TV, "I'm your boyfriend now, Nancy."

George looked over at Freddy, who was laughing, "Really? That is the best fucking line?" George continued to talk, "What year was this made, dude? Oh, my god, who fucking locks the inside of the house that you need a key to get out? So unrealistic!"

Freddy said, "I know, right? Wait, this is where Johnny Depp gets taken out."

"I can't believe this is Depp's first movie. I don't even recognize him; he's so young."

They finished the movie. George stared at Freddy with his mouth open in disgust. "Dude, you just wasted two fucking hours of my life."

"Consider it payback, bitch."

"How do ya figure?"

"Well, for starters, all the fucking golf tournaments you dragged me to. I hate golf."

"Yeah, well, that's why you're my caddy."

"Uh, caddy just translates to bitch that is wasting time."

"Whatever, see if I invite you to anything again."

"Oh, you will."

"Why, dude, you just shit on me."

"Cause you're a fucking giverrrr, remember?" he mocked.

"Very fucking funny, dude. You realize this movie is about a serial killer who pedophiled children, the parents kill him, and he comes back as Freddy fucking Kreuger? Then dices the parent's older kids all up? That's pretty fucking insane that you like this movie."

Freddy looked at him hard. He had a point, considering all that had happened to him revolving around a serial killer who kills children.

"Yeah, well, he didn't kill little children. They were fucking adults."

"Dude, high-school kids. Fuck, that is how you rationalize this? He had sexual acts with little children. That's fucked up in itself."

"I don't know, dude. This movie came out in 84. I was fucking five when I saw it. Just stuck with me. I'm sick in the head, what can I say?"

George held out his beer, "Aren't we all?" Freddy clinked his beer against his.

George said, "I guess it also helped to have the same fucking first name as his. Long live, Freddy." He held his beer out for another clink. Freddy obliged with an amen.

"You know," George continued, "the creepiest part of the movie was that seriously fucked up rhyme the kids sang in the background. You know, 1-2 Freddy's coming for you."

Just then, a text message alert sounded on Freddy's cell. He was smiling at George when he saw the sender's name; Jenny. He sobered up.

George said, "What's wrong?"

Freddy looked at him, "It's Jenny."

George's eyebrows shot up, "Fuck me."

Freddy read it first. He looked up in surprise. He relayed the message, "She's coming out for Labor Day weekend and wants to see me."

George leaned forward, "Dude, really?" He paused, "What are you gonna do?"

"What do you mean, what am I gonna do? I can't keep torturing myself that we're ever going to get back together. I can't see her."

"I think that's a good idea." He downed his beer and stood up. "Want another?"

"No, I'm good. I think I'm gonna take off."

"Yeah, okay. No problem." George hesitated, then gave Freddy his sexy look, "I had a good time tonight."

"Fuck you."

"I'm your fucking boyfriend now, Freddy," he mocked. "What? You're gonna deny me? Again?" Freddy walked away with his middle finger up. George responded as Freddy walked out the front door, "We're done! I'm totally over you! I'm gonna throw away the mixed tape I made for you!" The door closed.

Freddy sat in his car, looking at the text message. HI FREDDY.

I'M COMING OUT SEPT 1 TO SEE MY PARENTS. CAN WE TALK?

He hadn't responded yet. He typed in 'YES' but hesitated to send. He erased it. Threw his phone on the passenger seat and put his hand to his forehead. He whispered, "Don't fuck this up, Freddy."

He picked up his cell, logged in, and typed YEAH NAME TIME PLACE. I'LL BE THERE.

CHAPTER 19
JENNY

FREDDY LEANED IN close to the mirror and moved his head side to side, reviewing his freshly shaved face. "You've got this," he told himself. Then he smacked each cheek and growled, like a caveman heading off to get a woman. He wiped more fog away and stared at himself in the mirror. His entire chest and arms were covered in tattoos. Emblazoned across his chest in solid letters was the name Morris, in memory of the first body he had embalmed. He was thankful the man's last name wasn't Schwarzenegger. Freddy flexed his arms low with hands balled into fists. He checked for a bulge in his pecks. Still nothing. Oh well, Jenny wasn't about muscles. She was about personality, and that was certainly what he had. He leaned in closer to the mirror. "You fucked it up and left her alone." Freddy had lost so much with the murder of his daughter. He spiraled into a dark hole and didn't let anyone in. "It was your fucking fault. You bailed on her, dude." Jenny felt abandoned. She lost her daughter as well. Freddy smacked his cheek again. "You're going to get her back. Do you hear me? No fucking other dude is going to stand in your way." He checked the time on his cell lying on the counter. 4:51 pm. He knew the sun would set around seven.

Oceanside was a happening place on Saturday nights. Freddy parked in the nearby pay lot, put his ticket on the dash, and crossed the street to the restaurant bar, 333 Pacific. To his left was the famous Oceanside Pier, running almost two-thousand feet into the water. It was an iconic landmark in San Diego. Freddy admired the beauty, elated about having great weather for tonight. Surfers rode waves on either side of the pier. Spray from the water lifted behind them. A small number of clouds dotted the sky. Freddy knew the sunset was going to be perfect. He also knew sunsets were Jenny's favorite, always commenting on how they were paintings in the sky.

He checked his breath as he glided across the street and popped a breath mint to be on the safe side. Freddy felt pretty confident in his black button-up shirt and designer jeans. He left the top couple buttons undone, which revealed a hint of his chest tats, the lettering of Morris barely visible. His fohawk was meticulous. He had splashed on his cologne, Classic Lagerfeld, as it was Jenny's favorite; and part of his plan to woo her back into his arms.

The place was crowded—noise level like a rock concert. From high classed patrons with expensive attire to old men in Tommy Bahama shirts filled the place. The bar was lit up, orange spiral lights above brought a majestic ambiance. The long bar tables lit up with a coral blue undertone within their smoky glass tops. Bottles of alcohol stood resolute in the background awaiting the drink orders coming in. The inanimate objects, standing at attention, longed to assault the mouths and stomachs of patrons willing to do battle with them like MMA matches. To the left was the hustle and bustle of waiters and waitresses serving appetizers, drinks, and entrees to the luxurious tables with white linen. All the tables were full. People were waiting to be seated.

None of this mattered to Freddy. The earth stopped when he spotted her. The glow of her aura overwhelmed his senses, and every-thing else around him diminished into nothingness. Her blonde hair was straight, just below her shoulder blades. She wore a long summer dress, but it still had a look of sophistication and seduction as it clung to her body, highlighting the curves of her perky breasts. It had patterns in deep reds, blues, and hints of yellow. She stood at the bar watching the people around her. He could tell she was nervous. Thoughts of having her naked against his body began to invade his mind. He forced them back, took a deep breath, and walked to her. She caught his eyes, and he saw excitement. Her blue eyes sparkled in the light, matching the sparkle in the diamond earrings he had given her on their fifth anniversary. Freddy didn't miss a thing. An embalmer was all about the details.

"Hi, Freddy." She opened her arms to embrace him. They hugged. He held her tight.

Whispering as he held her, "Hi, Jenny."

They broke away, smiled, and fidgeted with their hands. Their eyes locked. All the sights and sounds drifted away into a blurry and deafened background. It had been a year since they had seen each other.

Freddy gently said, "I missed you."

She smiled. "It's been like, what…?"

"A year. The last time I saw you was at the courthouse."

She smiled but looked away.

Freddy said, "Drink?"

She nodded.

"Bartender!" He came over after pouring someone's drink. Freddy said, "She'll have the Southern Belle, and I'll have the White Tiger."

"Wow, you remembered," she said. She looked around the room, "I don't think we'll have a chance at a table."

Freddy smirked, "Our table is ready when you are."

She looked at him surprised, and then it dawned on her, "George?"

He frowned, "George? No, he doesn't even know about this. I can do stuff without George, you know." He paused, "Well, periodically, anyway."

She giggled. That giggle was like cold water in his face. It was his daughter's giggle. He coughed the sensation away. She didn't notice. Their drinks arrived.

He handed Jenny her drink, and he took his. "To new sunsets," he toasted.

She smiled, "To new sunsets."

Freddy loved her lips. They were not plump but elegant. He loved the way they felt in and on his mouth, remembering the soft, warmness of her smooth skin. He longed to kiss her again. Not yet.

"Come on," he said. He held out his hand for her to grab.

She grabbed it and followed him through the maze of people. He stopped at the hostess station, gave his name, and then heard the magical words of another hostess standing by, "Please follow me."

She guided them to a large plush horseshoe-shaped booth. It was beige with hints of orange backs on top of a bronze-colored bench. White linen, sparkling clean glasses and silverware, and a single lit candle in the middle finished the decor. Jenny scooted in on the left. He went to the right, and they met in the middle. The young female hostess handed them menus and said, "Your waiter will be with you shortly. Thank you for joining us at 333."

Jenny said, "Thank you." She then started perusing the menu.

Freddy took up the menu as well. "So, how was your flight?"

"Good."

"How are Mom and Dad?"

She looked up from the menu, "They're doing good, Freddy. They want to see you also."

Freddy looked at his menu, "Yeah, that would be nice. Maybe soon."

"What about tomorrow? They wanted me to ask. Dad's barbecuing."

Freddy grinned, "Wait, it's not his famous Costco burgers, is it?"

She laughed, "Of course. Nothing but the best."

"Well, then I'm in."

"Great. I'll text them now. Do you think George could make it?" She took out her cell from her black clutch purse.

"I'll see what he's up to. I always love to see him squirm, trying to hold back his curse words."

Freddy waited until she finished and put her phone away, "I thought you were coming out in November for Dad's birthday."

"I still am. I...I just decided to come out last minute for the holiday weekend."

The waiter arrived. He wore a pristine white collared shirt with the 333 Pacific title stitched in. He had black pants and a white knee-length apron. "Hello, my name is Jason. I'll be your waiter this evening. I apologize for the delay."

"Hello," Freddy responded, "No problem. It's a crazy night."

"Indeed, sir. Are you ready to order?"

He looked at Jenny and waited for the go-ahead look. She said, "He knows what I like."

"Okay," Freddy said, "Um," he scanned the entrees. "Uh, she will have the Mustard-Balsamic Glazed Salmon with a garden salad, ranch dressing on the side."

"Very good, sir. Great choice for the lady. And you?"

"I'll have the center cut filet."

"How would you like that cooked, sir?"

"Medium-well, please. And can we have the Ahi Bruschetta appetizer to start?"

"Very good. Is there anything else you would like?"

Jenny said, "Some water would be nice."

Freddy added, "We'll have another round of cocktails once we finish these as well."

"Very good. I will get your order in and be right back with the waters. Again, my name is Jason, and it's a pleasure to serve you this evening." He walked away.

She lifted her drink, eyebrows up, "Ooo-la-la, pleasure to serve you," she mocked.

Freddy lifted his glass and laughed. They took a sip and set them back down.

"You look stunning, by the way," Freddy said.

"Thank you and you're looking sharp."

"You want to walk the pier after dinner?"

"Sure. Looks like it will be a great sunset. I miss them."

"I miss you," Freddy let it slip out. He couldn't take the words back. He didn't want to.

She half-smiled and bit her lip. "So, how's work?"

He understood the deflection, "Busy. Two things certain in life. Death—"

"And taxes."

He lifted his glass. "Damn right." Took a sip. He set his drink down, "What about you? What have you been up to this last year?"

"Not much. I've been doing a little teaching at a tiny school. You know, part-time."

"Must be tough working part-time and paying the bills." Freddy began to fish for information. He wondered if she would tell him about the guy he heard in the background or if she planned to wait for the pier. Either way, he was ready to fight for her.

"Surprisingly, Boise is less expensive than I thought. You'd like it, Freddy."

"Is that an invitation?"

She smiled, "Nooo, I'm just saying you would like the nature. All the rivers and mountains, and the fresh air."

"Ah, but I would miss the smell of formaldehyde and death in the morning."

"Freddy, people are dying in Boise just the same."

"So you *are* inviting me."

"Whatever," she rolled her eyes and took another sip of her drink.

Jason, their waiter, showed up with their waters. "Here you go. Your appetizer should be here shortly." They nodded. Jason left.

Freddy said, "So I never heard what brought you out to Boise in the first place."

She set her drink down, "Do you remember Suzie?"

He thought about it, "She married that firefighter guy, right?"

"Yeah, then she divorced him, abuse stuff, and then moved to

Idaho. I stayed in contact with her over the years. She had an extra room."

"So you're still staying at her place?"

"Yes. She gave me free rent for a while. Dad's been sending me money to stay afloat."

Freddy smirked, "Daddy's little girl."

She smiled at that. "Don't be jealous."

"Oh, I'm being jealous, now?" he played. He reached over to tickle her side.

She flinched away, laughing, then whispered, "Stop it."

He pulled away, laughing. Touching her side brought a flood of memories. He remembered pulling the spaghetti straps of her shirt down off her shoulders, unclasping her bra the first time they made love in the backseat of her car. The touch of her bare skin was soft as a flower lightly brushed across his face. He remembered the honey-suckle perfume as he kissed her neck over and over. The sounds of her heavy breathing and slight moans echoed in his mind.

"Freddy? You okay?"

He snapped back to the restaurant, regained his composure, "Yeah, just thinking if I filed that paperwork Bob wanted me to file today. It's fine. I...I think I did."

"You sure. You seemed deep in thought there."

"Yeah, I'm fine."

The appetizer showed up. "Here you go, one Ahi Tuna Bruschetta," Jason said as he laid the pristine long white china plate down. Three beautifully layered pieces of ahi with edamame hummus, red pepper, and tomato, and topped with cilantro stood before them. "Bon appetit," Jason said.

"Thank you. Wow, that looks great."

Freddy took an appetizer plate and was about to put one on it when Jenny said, "Wait, I need to take a pic of that."

Freddy's hand retracted. He sighed, "Really? How many pictures of food do you have on your phone? I'm surprised you haven't run out of memory." He chuckled.

Her eyes flared wide at him, "As many as I want."

She was flirting with him. He watched her take the picture. She smiled at him—Her teeth bright white and perfect. He caught a glimpse of her tongue, so pink, so sweet, and remembered their first kiss. They were on the porch of her parent's home in San Marcos. They were making out when suddenly the front door opened, and her dad cleared his throat, "Jenny, time to come in." Mind you, they were in their mid-twenties.

"Freddy?"

He snapped back out of his memories again. "I'm here. Sorry."

"Are you sure you're okay?"

"Perfect." He dished up one of the appetizers for her then got one for himself. They ate.

"Oh, my god. This is so good," she said as she moaned in delight.

He loved everything about her. He regretted not fighting harder to keep her from running away. The evening went on. They ate, they drank, they talked, and laughed. But each of them steered clear of anything having to do with their daughter, Eve. She wasn't being ignored, but instead, their dinner together was being protected. If Evelyn had come up, then the night would have been a disaster. Right now, they remained within the eye of the hurricane. But inevitably, the storm was coming.

The check came and Freddy paid. They stepped outside and began to stroll toward the pier across the street from the restaurant. Palm trees dotted the view all along the coast as far as they could see. White sand beaches stretched out in both directions. People were swimming, surfing, and playing volleyball while food carts and vendors were busy filling orders. Throngs of people were walking the wooden pier and waiting to watch the sunset. Jenny clutched his arm. Freddy noticed and smiled.

He thought to himself, *"She is mine. I'm not going to lose her again."*

CHAPTER 20
THE SUNSET

6:44 PM. THE sun will set at 7:11 pm. Freddy and Jenny walked arm in arm. Couples lined both sides of the pier taking selfies, making out, watching the surfers, talking, eating ice cream, and staring into each other's eyes. The couples stood out to Freddy as he walked with his girl.

Jenny clutched his arm and put her head on his shoulder, "Thank you for meeting me tonight. I know it was short notice."

"My pleasure. I would do anything for you, Jenny."

They took their time walking. There was no rush.

Freddy said, "Hey, do you want to get a milkshake at Ruby's?"

She placed her hand on her stomach, scrunched her face, "I'm so full. I can't possibly put anything else in there."

"Yeah, you're right." Freddy didn't want the night to end. He knew the sunset would be the highlight. The sunset was the marker for the evening. It would be the finale. The hard talk was coming.

The smell of the sea mixed with the aroma of fish permeated the air. They passed the small general store for those who fished from the pier or wanted a souvenir. It was the midway point. At the far end was Ruby's Diner and the largest crowds. A fisherman just pulled up a two-foot sand shark causing many to stop, look, take a picture, and cheer the fisherman for a great catch. On the other side was a group of people trying to get close to a local pelican. It was always at the pier getting fed by the onlookers. Teenage girls screamed in unison as the pelican snapped at them when they got too close. It's large throat pouch extended out. The girls giggled in retreat, clutching each other.

They walked a little further. Now three-quarters down. Jenny pulled Freddy to the side at a rare clearing. "Let's watch the sunset from here," she said.

He didn't resist. He loved her taking the lead. He also knew this would be where the tough conversation would happen.

There was a light breeze. It was a warm night. Neither of them had jackets. They watched the large swells roll by them below and rise into surfable waves—each set leaving behind a trail of white foam.

Jenny said, "It's so beautiful."

"You're beautiful," Freddy countered.

She blushed with a quick glance at him, then returned her gaze on the horizon. The gold sunlight lit up her face. Her skin was glowing.

Jenny looked down at the water below and said his name in a serious tone, "Freddy."

He knew that tone. She had something to say. This was it. This was where she was going to tell him about the other guy. He wouldn't let her go. He stared at her.

She made eye contact, "I wanted to talk to you about something."

He didn't say anything. He waited. His eyes looking directly into hers. He masked a peaceful look while inside a volcano was ready to erupt. How was he going to react? How was he going to handle the truth of her being with another guy? Were they intimate? Worse, did he propose? Worse yet, did she say yes?

"Freddy…" she began but he jumped in.

He gently grabbed her arm, "Jenny, I don't care about the other guy. I don't care if he proposed. I don't care if you said yes." He stopped talking when he saw her face change from concern to holding back laughter. "That's what you wanted to tell me, right? That there's another guy in your life?"

She laughed, "Freddy, no. What?" She couldn't believe his train of thought. "How did you come up with that?"

"On the phone the other night. I heard a guy in the background."

She realized the moment he was talking about. "No, Freddy, that's Suzie's fiance."

Freddy tried to replay it back in his mind. All this time, he thought it was a guy saying 'honey' to her. But it was to Suzie.

Jenny giggled, "So this whole time you thought tonight was about that? Oh my god." She brought a hand to her mouth. "No, Freddy, I'm moving back home."

"What?" he responded. "Back home?"

"I've been doing a lot of soul searching. Talking with mom and dad. Talking with my therapist. All this time, I've been running away, Freddy." She paused, then put her hand out to caress his cheek. "I ran away from you."

His eyes became glassy with emotion. He swallowed, then said, "From me?"

Whispering, tears forming in her eyes, "Yes. I don't want to run anymore."

Freddy said, his voice cracking, "I'm never gonna lose you again, Jenny."

They kissed. It was passion, not from lust, but from the depths of their very being. Lovers who had fought through the darkness to find each other. Two people destined to be together regardless of the universe bent on their destruction. They had lost it all. There was nothing else to lose, everything to gain. Only two words could shatter this moment. Two words that could pierce their hearts.

A group of college kids nearby looking at their phones yelled out, "Angel Killer!"

CHAPTER 21
IT'S NOT OVER

THE ROOM WAS dark. It smelled like damp paper, musty, and moldy. Whiffs of death were caught in the lightly oscillating fan on top of a pile of books in the corner. An old twenty-inch boxed television was on. Grainy and unclear. It was the only source of light in the room, casting eerie shadows. A news anchor was reporting, "An arrest has been made this evening in the twenty-year-long killing spree of the Angel Killer. Just moments ago, detectives raided Carlos Ignasio's home in Lemon Grove. We don't have many details yet and are sending a team out now. We will have full coverage at 11 pm. In other news, we have…"

Steven Murdock tuned the rest out. He spoke towards the TV, "It is done." A year ago, he had buried key evidence on the property of Mr. Ignasio's home. Today, he called in an anonymous tip to authorities at a payphone outside of a 7-11.

"I did as you told me to." His voice sounded defeated. Pain suddenly shot down his arm. He grabbed it. His face soured. Spittle dripped from his mouth, "How long do I have?"

The pain subsided. He leaned his head back into his stained mustard-yellow recliner where the front corner slanted down broken many years ago. Steven sat in his Fruit-of-the-Loom underwear and nothing else. Large welts from what looked like spider bites dotted his pasty white inner thighs. Frozen dinners, half-eaten, stacked up next to him on the table, beer cans littered the floor. Newspapers and magazines were piled high along the edges of the living room. The curtains were drawn. Rods not level. Fabric torn in some places. Steven couldn't smell the rancid odor of rotting meat anymore. He was immune.

He tried to peer behind himself while yelling, "Mom, shut up! I don't want to hear it." No one was talking to him. His was the only voice to be heard in the trailer. He pushed his smudged eyeglasses further up on the bridge of his nose. Frustrated, he turned again, "Just shut up! I can't hear dad while you're blabbing!" The TV light reflected off of his glasses. Shadowy figures sat back behind him in the recesses of the darkness. He rested his eyes as he relaxed back into the recliner.

Suddenly, Steven's eyes flared open. He jerked forward off the recliner. Horror and fear were upon his face. He started to cry. It was a dry cry. "I'm sorrrryyyy," he croaked. He began to crawl toward the figures in the back room of the trailer. "I'm soorrrrrryyyy. I didn't meeeaaaannn it." Steven was in utter fear of what he approached. Unable to stand. Stacked cans toppled as he crawled by. A pile of books fell on top of him as his legs bumped into them. "Dad, forgive me."

He got closer and closer. Two outlines of people sat upright in the bed. They were draped in a stained, sheer fabric. Steven lifted himself to his knees with the help of the bed. "Dad, please," he begged. "Mom just made me so mad. I'm sorry."

Steven reacted like someone was scolding him. "Okay, I will," he paused. "Mom, I'm sorry. Forgive me."

He flinched backward like someone was going to hit him, "I'm sorry, sorry, okay, sorry, I will, sorry." Coming back to his knees, breathing heavily, he said, "Mom, truly, I mean it. I'm so sorry for yelling at you. I'm stupid!" He slapped his face hard. "Please, mom, forgive me."

Steven waited for a long moment until he finally let out a sigh of relief. His apology was accepted by a voice only he could hear. Then shock hit him once again, "But Dad, I said I was sorry." Steven listened to an unknown response. "Dad, please no. I said I was sorry."

He slowly crawled to the counter. He reached up and felt around. He found it. The metal object scraped on the counter as he dragged it to the edge. Steven put his back to the cabinet and opened up his legs, looking at the two figures representing his mom and dad. His eyes pleaded for them to stop. Steven held out the object in his hand. It was tweezers with rust invading the dull silver metal. He took the tweezers and proceeded to bring them to his inner thigh. The welts were not caused by spiders. They were tweezer bites caused by his own hand. Steven screamed as he grabbed hold of the white, pasty meat of his skin and twisted. The skin ripped off and he held it before his pain laced face. His shaky hand placed the tool back onto the counter. His arm fell to his side while he cried.

As if someone was yelling at him, he responded, "I...I...I'm not crying."

He stood on shaky legs, "Yes, sir." His face looked down. Then he slowly looked up at mom and dad. His lip began to curl into a half-smile, nodding. His voice was stronger, sinister as he said, "Yes, sir. It will be done."

Steven entered the bathroom. The toilet seat was up. Crusted feces stained the rim. Stained porcelain under the murky water. The mirror above the sink was shattered from when he hit it years ago. The once white sink was a stained yellow with splotches of dried blood and toothpaste.

A moldy, yet clear shower curtain with faded rubber duckies was bunched to the side. A dark rim of dirt left behind from past baths remained in the tub. Rust was around the handles and plug. A towel covered a small box next to the bathtub with squeaking noises coming from beneath. He ripped it away to reveal two rats inside a cage. One was black with gray spots while the other was cream-colored. Both squeaked louder from the sudden removal of the towel.

Steven started to run the water. He sat on the edge and pushed the plug down so the water wouldn't drain. It began to fill, dislodging the particles of dirt and pubic hair left behind from the last bath. Standing, he pulled his underwear off and waited. Lost in the sound of the water, he stared into the tub. Steven's right hand crept up to his chest, placing it over his heart.

One of the rats screeched, wiggling in his grasp after plunging his right hand inside the cage. Its eyes almost popped out from the strength of his grip. Steven reached to the counter and grabbed hold of an old, rusty fishing knife. He stretched out his arms over the bath and then stuck the knife into the stomach of the rat. The knife cut downward, releasing blood and innards into the water. He squeezed all the juices from the animal and tossed it into the trash where several other rat carcasses lay. Maggots and flies were disturbed.

Steven stepped into the bath and submerged his body into the bloody water. Only his pudgy face stayed above, his cheeks like floatation devices. His eyes closed. Darkness. Droplets from the spigot sounded like thuds within his mind. His mind flashed to sporadic memories from each drop. Every memory in a rose-colored fog.

Dad by his door. Dad yelling. Dad pulling Steven's pants down. Dad spanking. Dad pulling his own pants down. Dad raping him. Mom watching at the doorway.

Steven calmed his mind. His eyes opened wide. He whispered, "Yes, Lord. It's not over."

CHAPTER 22
COSTCO BURGERS

TWO BEERS CLINKED together. "They fucking got'em, dude," George said and then took a swig.

"I can't believe it," Freddy responded while mechanically taking a drink.

Jenny wore a yellow sundress and was talking to her mom and dad over by the barbeque. Freddy watched her laugh out loud. Her dad must have said another one of his jokes while Mrs. Carrino said, "Oh, Ron, stop it."

George said, "So, what's going on with Jenny?"

"She's moving back home."

"Fuck me. She's moving back to your place?"

"No, asshole, she's moving in here."

"Oh. Yeah, right. Sorry." He took another swig.

George noticed Freddy never took his eyes off of her. "Is she naked yet?"

Freddy's eyes looked at him. He shrugged his shoulders, froze them in place, had his hands out, beer in hand, "What the fuck are you talking about?"

"You've been undressing her since you got here, dude. You need to play it cool, like me. Watch and learn."

George turned and yelled, "Hey, Mrs. and Mr. Carrino!" They stopped their conversation with Jenny and looked at him. "Thanks for the invite. Truly appreciate it. This has warmed my heart." He placed his hand holding his beer over his heart and tapped his chest. Then bowed slightly.

They smiled. Mr. Carrino said, "Good to see you again, George. We're glad to have you."

George turned to Freddy. "See, now watch Jenny." Freddy was looking past George right at her. "She's now listening to her mom comment about how sweet I am." Freddy watched her mom's mouth almost verbatim say these exact words. "I also fucking landed extra points from the dad. Now there's a chance you'll fucking lose the love of your life...to me. Cheers."

Freddy smiled, and they clinked beers. "I'm lost without you, buddy. But, you would have a better chance of embalming me than getting Jenny. Cheers."

They clinked beers again. "We'll see." George winked.

George said, "Hey, I landed the site in Vista, by the way. See, it pays to hang out with the mayor after all."

Freddy didn't respond as his eyes were not focused on George. His friend, however, followed Freddy's vision and was surprised to see the same locked eyes returned by her. The look of love. He whispered, "Mother fucker."

He turned back to Freddy, "So where were you last night?"

Freddy was surprised by the question, "Working, what do ya mean?"

"Working, huh?"

"Yeah, working. What were you doing?"

"Ah, deflection. Good one."

"What are you fucking talking about, dude?"

"Man, you are good. My student is coming along nicely. Deflection and then blame. Love it." George brushed Freddy's shirt while leaning back a bit in appreciation of his protege.

Mr. Carrino yelled out, "Burgers are almost ready, everyone!"

It was a nice squared off backyard with some grass and a covered patio overlooking the golf course behind their home. It was a typical gated community located on the greens of St. Mark Golf Club. George and Freddy stood by the back gate to the course while the others stayed under the patio shade. Mrs. Carrino hurried through the sliding doors to get things ready in the kitchen. Jenny waved, "Bring it in, boys!"

Freddy began to walk toward her. George leaned in and whispered, "You should've told me you guys got back together, bro. Now it's gonna be really fucking awkward at the din-din table." Freddy froze, and George walked over to Jenny. "Can't wait to feast!"

Freddy said under his breath, "Fuck." George was a bloodhound for the awkward moments. Freddy prepared himself.

Like Tony the Tiger, George yelled, "Smells GREEAAATTT!"

They each loaded their plate with a burger, chips, potato salad, and string bean casserole. Outside on the patio, they sat at the glass table.

"So, George, what have you been up to these days?" Mr. Carrino asked.

"Well, sir, thank you for asking. I've expanded 'Hang In There' to two more states, and locations have been popping up all over California."

"Wow, what states did you take over?" Jenny mocked.

George smiled, "Nevada and Arizona."

Mr. Carrino said, "Who would have thunk people would like to climb indoors." Then he and his wife laughed.

"Well," George countered, "it's more like a gym. We use climbing exercises and the walls more like a workout and preparation for those who want to take it to the great outdoors."

"Good to know. And Freddy, how are you doing?"

"Doing good, sir."

"Sir? What happened to dad?"

Freddy looked at Jenny, who gave him a shy smile. Freddy looked around the table nervously. "Um, doing good, dad." He chuckled. "It's been a while," he added.

"Yes, too long." He took a sip of his drink and made eye contact with Jenny. She gave him a playful smile.

George noticed the two love-birds' hidden exchange and grinned. "Jenny, welcome back. When did you get in?"

"I flew in Thursday night and head back Tuesday."

"And just hanging out with the folks the last couple of days?" He was fishing.

Freddy wanted to kick him under the table, but it was a smokey glass top, and they would see it. He instead gave up as he knew George would not relent. In a louder than normal voice, he said, "Jenny and I had dinner last night, alright?"

Silence engulfed the table. "Well, hot-damn!" George said with a big grin and slapping Freddy on the shoulder hard, "That's fantastic. I'm glad you guys got some chit-chatting in together."

Jenny gave George the "really?" look.

Mrs. Carrino lifted the plastic pitcher up and said, "Anyone want some ice-tea?"

"I would love some, thank you, Mrs. C," George responded in his I-won-smart-ass attitude.

There was definitely an awkward time together as they ate and had small talk. Jenny and Freddy hadn't officially told anyone yet.

Freddy said, "Your burgers are amazing, dad. Are you ever going to tell us the secret recipe?"

He smiled, "If I did, then I would have to kill ya."

Everyone chuckled at the table, most forcefully chuckling as that was his patent answer to that particular question. Everyone at the table knew it was just plain ordinary frozen Costco burgers but played along anyway.

Mrs. C stood, "How about some dessert? I made brownies." She didn't wait for a response and automatically made her way inside to fetch the tray.

"Thanks, mom," Jenny said as the plate of brownies was set down in the middle. Jenny continued, "I think this is the best time to say it."

Everyone froze in place.

"Freddy and I are working on getting back together."

"Holy shit!" George exclaimed. "That's fucking awesome!"

"George!" Mrs. C said sharply.

"Oh, sorry."

Mr. Carrino said, "That is great, guys. Really happy to hear this. It blesses your mom and me so much."

Jenny added, "But in order to move forward, we all need to talk together, so it's not awkward. We all suffered a great loss, and Freddy and I don't want anyone walking on eggshells."

Everyone nodded in agreement.

"Mom and dad, tell us how you're feeling and whatever else you want to add."

Taken aback by being the first to talk, Dad led the charge, "Well, I know that these last couple years have been hard on everyone. It's been hard on us. We lost our granddaughter," he began to choke up and put his hand to his mouth. Mom rubbed his shoulder. He lowered his hand and looked directly at Freddy, "but we also lost a son." He couldn't talk.

Freddy fought back tears and felt a lump in his throat.

Mom said, "I've been fighting depression these last couple of years, and it's been really hard on my...husband," her voice cracked. She also fought to keep her emotions at bay. "I blamed myself for not being able to take Eve that day."

"Mom, it wasn't your fault."

Mrs. Carinno held up her hand, "No, dear, let me finish. I blamed myself, right or wrong, but I feel the presence of Eve helping to guide us back together. She is still with us." She fell into dad's awaiting arms and buried her face in his chest, crying. Jenny, sitting beside her, caressed her arm.

"Mr. and Mrs. C," George began. "I just want to say you have been a great influence in my life. I had good parents, but I didn't have great parents. And you guys fall in the bracket of great." They acknowledged him with nods of appreciation. Mrs. C was wiping away tears with her napkin. "I melted the day Eve called me Uncle G." George was getting emotional now. "And losing her...was, I'm sorry Mrs. C, the worst fucking thing ever. It hit me hard. I had to be there for Freddy. He's my best friend, and to see him lose Eve, for us all to lose her, was... beyond anything imaginable. Many times I still think it's not real. Like it never happened. Like she's in the other fucking room. Sorry." He held up his hands, apologetic for the language to Mrs. C. She half-smiled. "Anyway, the two of you getting back together just...just...I don't know. It just says screw you, world. You tried to take us all out, but you didn't win." His voice lowered, "You didn't win."

Freddy grabbed his friend's shoulder in appreciation and said, "You didn't win."

All of them began to say, "You didn't win."

George said, "I love you, guys."

"Aww," Mrs. C said, "We love you too, George."

They stood and hugged. Freddy put his arm around Jenny's waist. "I want to say thank you for being with each of us as we walked through this together and separately. Your support was monumental. And your continued support for what is coming will be huge for us. Jenny and I still need to talk through some things, work things out, and see where it goes. So, thank you."

They all hugged again.

Jenny said, "One last thing, I don't want any of you to not feel comfortable talking about...well, you know, the Angel Killer. There is going to be a lot of news. Maybe even some media coverage of us. I just want you all to know that he has no power over us."

Mrs. Carrino said one final thing, "I hope they hang that fucker!"

Everyone's eyes opened in surprise, having never heard mom say a curse word in her life.

George laughed, "Well done, Mrs. C, well done." He lifted his beer in salute.

CHAPTER 23
EVELYN ANN FOLEY

FREDDY TOOK MONDAY off to spend with Jenny before she returned to Boise to button things up there. The family decided to all pay a visit to Eve's grave. She was buried at Pinewood, where Freddy works, in Oceanside. Freddy thought he would be able to embalm his daughter, but last minute decided against it. A colleague of his who won last year's Embalmer of the Year award came in and took care of Eve.

Jenny stared at the grave marker.

'EVELYN ANNE FOLEY'

4-4-2009 to 3-17-2014

Our giggle-bug

"Hi, Eve," she whispered. Freddy stood behind her. She put her hand out toward Freddy. Freddy grabbed it and stepped next to her. "I brought daddy with me. We're both here."

In the distance, Mr. and Mrs. Carrino stood with George. Eve's grave was at the top of a low hill. There was a spectacular view of the Camp Pendleton mountains along with Palomar Mountain range just beyond. The sun was out. A fresh breeze was blowing as a slight haze settled on the horizon.

Freddy said, "Hi giggle-bug." Jenny noticed the sincerity of his voice. It wasn't as if he was talking just to appease her but as though he actually believed he was talking directly to Eve. Freddy had always seen death black and white. He believed we were born and when we die there's nothing else, just darkness. She looked at him, surprised. Freddy smiled and squeezed her hand.

They stood there for a long while at her grave—no words—just holding hands looking at Eve and the view beyond.

Freddy said, "Do you remember when she came home from school so mad?"

"Which time?" she mused.

He smiled, "Yeah, no, it was when she learned how to spell her name."

"Oh," she chuckled, recalling the memory. "Yes, *that* time."

He continued, "We asked her what happened, and she said she didn't like her middle name. Why, honey? 'It's stupid,' she said. You told her it was a beautiful middle name. 'It's not normal,' she kept saying. We went on and on for days until you found her writing paper and saw that she was spelling her middle name A N D. I loved seeing her face light up once we explained it to her."

Jenny snuggled up next to him. "Yeah, she was amazing."

Freddy said, "Cause you're amazing."

She squeezed him tighter. They held each other as they stared at Eve's grave.

Freddy said, "Jenny, I…"

She pulled away to look at him. "What is it?"

"It's hard to say, really. I…I don't even know…"

"No secrets. Just let it out. We all need to do that."

He looked at her. His face was serious. "I tried to raise her."

Her face became perplexed, "Raise her?"

"I tried to raise her back from the dead."

Her head craned backward in confusion.

He continued, "Well, not her but the other girl and when George and I—"

"George was with you?"

"Yeah, I saw Eve or a ghost of Eve...I don't know. I don't even know how to talk about this shit."

Her hands gestured, "Okay, um, just start from the beginning. Like who was the girl?"

"It was the Angel Killer's last one. George helped me pick her up at the crime scene. We pulled over at a private lot and..."

"And what?"

He took a deep breath, "Wait, um, I need to go back a bit to explain. I heard this guy on the radio talking about a story in the Bible."

"The Bible? Youuu," she said, stretching the word out.

"Yeah, crazy. I'm gonna have to tell you about Alice Cooper. Anyway, I heard this story that night they announced the murder. They said that if you believe in Jesus, then you can raise the dead." He answered her surprise, "I know, right?"

He continued, "I know it's crazy, I'm crazy. I just...I don't know. It was something inside of me just saying go for it. I'm an all-in type of guy. Anyway, I arranged the pick-up, met George, and that's what happened."

She timidly asked, "What happened?"

"Nothing happened. I saw Eve's ghost, or maybe it was just my fucked-up imagination. Nothing happened. We took the girl's body to the Medical Examiner and went home. Jenny, I just thought if there was a chance then..."

"She's gone, Freddy. You have to stop all of this if *us* is going to happen. I can't take any more stakeouts or vigilante crap. Now add in dead-raising? I can't take it. None of it."

"I know. They caught the guy, so no need to do any of that stuff. I know she's gone. I know. Really, I do."

Jenny added, "And we need to continue therapy."

"Really? It's over, Jenny. Let's just start fresh."

"No, we can't start fresh and go on as if nothing happened."

His voice raised a bit, "I didn't say nothing happened. I'm just saying, why continue talking about all the bullshit with some stranger who doesn't care about us. They only want the money."

"Cause, Freddy, this bullshit is what caused our divorce in the first place."

"That's not fair."

"It's not? You're the one who threw the chair into the glass window at the office—that mom and dad paid for, by the way."

"They did? Why didn't you say something?"

"I tried, Freddy. You weren't listening to anyone. You went off into your own little world."

Freddy spun, hands flailing, "Oh, my little world. See, that's how you view things, Jenny. Everything is in a pretty little box with a bow on it. It's not that simple."

Jenny stared at him. He stared back.

George yelled up the hill, "Hey, who wants ice cream? My treat!"

Freddy relented, "Okay, fine. I'll continue to see a therapist. But for how long?"

"As long as it takes, Freddy."

"That could be our entire fucking lives, Jenny."

"Well, if that is what it takes, then we need to do it."

"What if I don't need it, Jenny."

She scoffed, "It's always about you."

"That's not what I said."

"It's what you don't say, Freddy."

"What do you want from me!"

George yelled again, trying to be lighthearted, "Ice cream!"

"I want you to be my husband. I want you to fight for me."

"I was, and I did."

"No, you let me run away."

"I thought you wanted space."

"I didn't know what I wanted, but you let me go."

"Jenny, I couldn't fucking function with Eve gone."

"Oh, and I could? See, this is what I'm talking about."

"Guys," George called, "ice cream, you know, it's cold, and delicious, and fun?"

Jenny relaxed, "I'm gonna leave Idaho. I'm coming home in November. The only question is who's home am I coming back to."

He didn't respond.

She took that as his answer. "Fuck off, Freddy."

"Jenny, hey," he tried to grab her arm, but she shook it away and stormed down the hill. He called after her, "Jenny, don't do this. I just need time to process."

She passed George on her way down. George said, "Jenny." She flipped him off. "Oh, okay, yeah, we'll talk later."

Mr. and Mrs. C held their daughter and got into their car. Ron waved goodbye to George and Freddy with a concerned fatherly look on his face. The situation was dire.

George walked up to Freddy, who looked at the view. He stood next to his best friend. No words were exchanged.

George finally said, "Actually, ice cream sounds pretty good."

CHAPTER 24
PARALLEL LINES

"WHERE YA GOING, dude?" George asked as Freddy passed him.

"Work."

George threw up his hands and said to himself, "What the fuck is happening?" He turned to look at the beautiful mountains, and then he turned to Eve's grave. "You want ice cream, right?" As if Eve responded to him, he said, "Well, at least someone wants ice cream around here." He shook his head and headed down the slope. Freddy walked through the graveyard toward the buildings in the distance. George opened his car door, but before getting in, he yelled, "I'm fucking getting ice cream!"

Freddy entered through the employee kitchen. The microwave light flickered as always. Mack, the maintenance guy, popped up from behind the opened fridge door with a yogurt cup. "Hey, Freddy."

Freddy passed him and said, "Ever gonna fix the microwave light?"

Mack closed the fridge, "Uh, yeah, sure."

Freddy went directly to his office and retrieved his personal embalming tools. The black leather zipped case was thin and light-weight. He slammed the drawer closed and left the room. The embalming room was devoid of any cadavers, but the fluorescent lights lit up the space. He went to the counter and opened up his kit. A metal highchair with wheels was situated next to him. With one hand, he pulled the chair over without looking while his other hand flipped the case open.

STEVEN MURDOCK SAT inside his shed. A single light above his head swayed ever so gently. Darkness surrounded him on the edges as he sat at his dirty workbench. An assortment of knives rested inside a black leather strip. He strummed his fingers across them, mesmerized by the sparkling stainless steel.

FREDDY RAN HIS fingers across his tools. His eyes stared, trance-like, at the dissecting forceps, hooks, curved needles, serpentine needles, scissors, and scalpels. He understood each of them intimately. Their function, their purpose.

STEVEN PULLED OUT one knife and began to stroke the blade along the sharpening rod he held in his other hand. The scratching and scraping of the blade brought ecstasy to his mind and body. He started slowly at first, then gradually built into a frenzy as pornographic images flashed within his mind.

FREDDY PULLED OUT one of his dissecting forceps and began to wipe it with a polishing cloth. All of his tools were pristine, but it didn't matter. He cleaned the instruments almost daily and, of course, after every embalming. It was more than just a duty. It was his bliss. It calmed him.

STEVEN FINISHED THE sharpening of the Elk Ridge hunting set. He unbuckled his belt and slid it out of the loops of his pants. Placing it upside down, he smiled satisfactorily at the fifteen lines he had scratched in with a knife. He pulled out his pocketknife and marked a new line for the last angel he had recently birthed. The media only knew of fourteen. The other two they never found, but it didn't matter. Birthing angels wasn't about the media. It was about mercy. Transcendence for the children chosen by god.

FREDDY FINISHED CLEANING. He opened up a front pouch and slid out a leather notebook wrapped in a cord. Unwinding it, he opened it to see the history of all of his embalming's throughout his career. He treated each decedent with the utmost respect. They were sons, daughters, mothers, fathers, grandparents, each having a story. The body was empty, but he saw the body as a vessel that once carried an entity. Regardless of their life choices, he would never know, nor cared to know. He still embalmed them like royalty.

STEVEN TUCKED HIS shirt in, zipped up his pants, placed his belt back through the loops, and buckled it. He pulled out his favored blade and inspected it, twisting it back and forth in front of his face. The light caught on the stainless steel and flashed on his face. This was the blade used to form the angel wings. Delicate, thin, and precise. For most, a hunter's blade for skinning animals. For Steven Murdock, a disciple's blade for birthing angels.

FREDDY OPENED UP a small velvet pouch tied inside his instrument case. He pulled out what looked like a thimble. It was his customized embalming blade. A leather-encased thimble with a razor-sharp slightly curved blade attached. It resembled a claw. Freddy used this instrument to sever the carotid artery before pumping the body with embalming fluids. It was his special tool. A representation of his favorite movie, *A Nightmare on Elm Street*, a nod to the infamous Freddy Krueger character. He saw the movie at the age of five with his dad because he had the same first name.

STEVEN PULLED THE string of the overhead light, casting the entire shed in darkness. He stared into the void and waited. Ten minutes, twenty. At the thirty-minute mark, he heard whispers within his mind. But to him, they were not in his mind; they were real. The whispers told him things. Told him places. Told him which children to look for. It was a cacophony of chaotic voices calling out to him. "Give me ears to hear you," Steven whispered. He closed his eyes and concentrated. Several more minutes passed. He reached and pulled the light on. His eyes flared open. He nodded, "It will be done."

FREDDY LOOKED AT the three decedents in the fridge, ready to be embalmed. He pulled the chart of the one nearest him. Paul Kingsly. Died of lung cancer. Funeral scheduled for this weekend. "Well, Mr. Kingsly, it is a pleasure to meet you today. I know you had a rough ending, but I assure you, you will receive the red-carpet treatment under my care. Your loved ones looking upon you this weekend will see you healthy and remember you full of life." He looked at the chart again under special instructions. The wife asked to make sure Paul had a grin on his face for viewing. Freddy nodded, "It will be done."

CHAPTER 25
HAPPY BIRTHDAY

EORGE CASEY'S HOME was packed. It was Friday night, October 14th. The band was about to go live. The three-panel sliding glass doors were open, connecting the massive living room to the outdoor patio and pool area. The stage was positioned between the two areas. Bartenders were serving drinks to the people surrounding the full bar. Others formed groups in front of the stage and pool area with drinks in hand. House music played in the background while the band continued with their soundcheck, first with each instrument and then each vocal. People were dressed to the nines in suits, tuxedos, and ballroom dresses. An ice sculpture of George flexing was the centerpiece outside. To the side was a pile of gift bags and a basket of cards.

The long-haired rocker's effort to get everyone's attention created a loud high-pitch squeal that caused many to whimper and cover their ears. "Hello, everyone! Are you guys ready to rock?" A semi-loud cheer went up. "George, I thought you said you had cool fucking friends." George shrugged and laughed. Others laughed as well. The rocker said, "Hey, are you guys ready to celebrate George's birthday?" The place erupted in screams and yells of appreciation. "We're Wasting June. Hit it!" The electric guitar ignited, then the drums kicked in. The sultry vocals of the lead singer with a simple puke-green t-shirt that said 'Suck

It' on the front began to fill the air. "Sweet mother's cherry pie. Tastes divine…"

George was talking to a man and woman, "I love this fucking band. Did you know I'm their agent? I found them at the Casbah in San Diego last year. Love this guy's voice, Tommy Modifica." They nodded and smiled. George spotted Freddy coming through the open doors. George ditched the people, "Hey, sorry, I gotta go."

"Freddy, what the fuck? About time," George charged. Freddy smiled, and they bear-hugged.

"Happy birthday, buddy."

"Thanks. Hey, Wasting June just started. Want a drink?"

"Yeah."

"Come on. Let me introduce you to Alicia, the bartender," George growled. "She's fucking hot."

Freddy countered, "Do you know any ugly people?"

"Yeah, I know you," he grinned.

Freddy got in line to get his drink. George got scooped up in multiple hellos and quick conversations as he was the birthday boy party favorite. Waiters in black and white attire walked the area with hors d'oeuvres on silver platters. One waiter had champagne and wine. Freddy quickly snatched one then walked through the crowd of people in front of the band. He wanted to get to the pool area. He needed fresh air.

Mumbling under his breath, "You got to be fucking kidding me." Freddy saw the larger-than-life ice sculpture of his friend.

George startled him, "Like it?"

Freddy shook his head in unbelief.

"Don't be jealous. I'll get one made for your fucking birthday in a couple weeks."

"Don't you dare!"

"Kidding!" He laughed. "I know you hate parties. Not even sure why I'm fucking friends with you."

"I'm the one with the smarts in this relationship."

"Yeah, that's why I have all the fucking money, and you don't."

"I've got plenty of money. You just don't let me spend it."

"I just like to take care of my women, is all."

They laughed.

George noticed his drink, "What the fuck is that?"

"What? It's champagne."

"You need a real drink. Those are for the children."

The crowd applauded the end of a song. Another song started. George instantly recognized it and yelled out, "Love this fucking song!"

Tom, the lead singer, said, "Thank you, George. Apparently, you're the only one who does." Everyone laughed. "This is called 'Nurse Ratchet.'" The guitars kicked in. Drums blasted. Tom sang. More cheers. Liquor was flowing. People were beginning to loosen up. Some started dancing.

George said, "Hey, let's get that fucking drink."

"I'm fine. Really."

George gave him a serious look showing his displeasure.

"Really, I'm good."

"You're not good. I can tell." He tapped his own forehead with his index finger.

"George, seriously, I'm good. Go on. Enjoy your party, man. It's your fucking birthday."

"You sure? I can introduce you to—"

"No," he cut him off, "I'm sure. I'm good. Go."

George stared at him for a long moment.

"Just fucking go, dude. We'll make out later."

"Promise?"

"Just fuck off!"

George slowly backed away and flipped him off while smiling. "I'll come for you later."

Freddy walked to the balcony on the patio overlooking the ocean. A private staircase descended down to the beach. The waves crashed on the shore a hundred feet below. It was high-tide, and the white foam of the crashing waves had a slight fluorescent glow to them.

"Not in the mood to party either?" a woman said to his left. She was wearing a red silk dress that draped down to the floor. Diamond earrings and necklace sparkled in the light. Her breasts wanted to bust out of the confined bodice. "I'm Melody."

"Freddy."

"I know."

Freddy squinted, "I apologize if we met before."

"No, I just know of you from the media."

"Ahh," Freddy understood. "Yes, the family fucked over by the Angel Killer." He took a drink of his champagne as he looked off into the darkness of night.

"I'm sorry, I didn't mean to..."

"It's fine. I'm used to it."

"Is your ex-wife here?"

Freddy looked at her, puzzled, "No. She is not."

"I just heard she was back in town."

"Who the fuck are you?" he snapped.

"I'm a journalist for the Union."

"Now it fucking makes sense." He began to walk away.

She quickly said, "You know they're not sure it's the actual Angel Killer they caught, right?"

Freddy stopped in his tracks, turned, "What the fuck are you talking about?"

"It's just...my sources are saying they're not sure."

"What are you trying to do right now? Like how does this information help me whatsoever?"

"I just thought I'd see how you felt about that?"

Freddy said in disgust, "Fuck off, lady. That's how I feel." He walked away.

Freddy wanted to leave the party. He started making his way through the crowd in front of the band when suddenly, George jumped onto the stage, grabbing the mic which screeched. George said, "Ouch!" He put his finger in his ear and wiggled it while scrunching his face. He smiled and said, "Where is Freddy?"

Freddy was almost through to the other side, heading for the front door. He stopped. All eyes focused on him. "There you are. Come up here," George commanded.

Freddy hesitated.

George said, "Now, motherfucker." The crowd laughed.

Freddy slowly made his way to the stage. He felt very uncomfortable. George pulled him to stand next to him, then slung his arm over his shoulder and embraced him. "This fucking guy is my best friend." The crowd cheered. "He literally saved my ass. I was depressed, broke, depressed, and did I say, broke." The crowd laughed. "When everyone said I was a loser, this guy said what?" George pushed the mic in Freddy's face.

Freddy cautiously said, "You're a dickhead?" The crowd laughed louder.

"No fuck-face, you said why do you worry about what others think, just go for it."

Freddy leaned in, getting more comfortable, "Oh, yeah, that's what I said." The crowd laughed.

George said, "Freddy gave me a thousand dollars. He never expected it back. Side-note, I'm never giving it back." Crowd chuckled. "What I want to say is thank you, my friend, for believing in me. For not allowing me to give up. For investing in me even though you probably thought it was a crazy idea that wouldn't work."

Freddy leaned in, "I still don't think it's gonna work." The crowd chuckled.

"Well, my friend," George looked at him with a serious face, "Thank you. Truly, thank you." The crowd erupted in cheers. The drummer hit a few beats.

Freddy said, "Can I go now, Dad?"

George smiled, "I have a gift for you."

Shocked, Freddy responded, "It's not my birthday. It's yours."

"Yeah, it's my fucking birthday, and I'll do what I want to." The crowd chuckled. George pulled out an envelope. "Here."

Freddy said, "What is this, dude?"

"Just fucking open it."

Freddy slowly opened the white envelope while staring at his friend. His best friend. He looked down and pulled out a ticket. He read it. Admission to the Cinespia's October 22nd showing of *A Nightmare on Elm Street* at the Hollywood Forever Cemetery in Los Angeles. Freddy gasped, "No fucking way."

Suddenly the lights dimmed in the house, and four girls wearing thong bikinis carried in a sheet cake with sparkler candles sizzling on top. The traditional happy birthday song groaned to life, and everyone joined in. Freddy and George's face were on top of the cake. Instead of George blowing out the candles, the four girls did the honors with their pouty lips, butts sticking out as they leaned in. They walked away, setting the cake down on an awaiting table .

George said, "Surprise! Happy birthday, Freddy. This party is for both of us, my friend."

George gave the mic back to Tom. The lead singer smiled and then began a new song, "This one is called 'Pretty Little Poison Vial of Death' and goes out to the birthday boys. Happy fucking birthday." They blasted the song. More cheers, more dancing, more drinking.

Freddy and George stepped off the stage and to the side. Freddy said, "Dude, what just happened?"

"You happy?"

"I was happy before this."

"Fucking liar. Seriously, dude, I'm so for you. And I'm so thankful for you." They hugged.

They pulled away. Freddy said, "I can't believe you got those tickets. That is fucking amazing. You're going, right?"

"Yeah, I'm fucking going. I love cemeteries and fucking cheesy 80's movies."

Freddy's face became serious. His emotions on edge, "Thank you, George. Seriously."

George lightly hit his friend's chest with the back of his hand, "Of course, my friend. I love you, dude. Good things ahead."

"Yeah, good things ahead."

George suddenly grabbed someone's drink right out of their hand, turned to the crowd, and yelled at the top of his lungs, "I'm a fucking giverrrrr! Let's party!!!" He chugged the drink, handed the empty glass back to the man, and ran into the dancing crowd.

"I fucking love Wasting June!!!" he yelled. He took off his tie and wrapped it around his head like a Japanese Samurai. Tom echoed back, "And we love you, George!" The crowd cheered.

Freddy watched his friend. He looked back down at the ticket in his hand. Inside the envelope, he spotted something folded. He pulled it out. It was a check for one-thousand dollars, made out to him. In the memo, it said, "Thank you for believing in me."

CHAPTER 26
THE DRIVE

FREDDY'S CELL PHONE buzzed. It was a text message from an unknown number. "ITS ALICE. JUST THINKIN ABOUT CONVO WE HAD. HOPE YOU'RE DOING WELL."

Freddy saved his number, then looked at the message over and over. He recalled the Narnia talk they had at the hotel. Something happened to him from the plane ride home, but the feeling went away as time went on. When he read Alice Cooper's message, however, the feeling came back.

He thought about texting back but couldn't find the words. He was going to just tell him he was good, but his instincts said not to lie. Then an internal battle of what to say ensued. Hi Alice. Other than losing my daughter to the Angel Killer, my ex-wife getting back with me, then leaving me, now I'm off to see a movie at a cemetery. I'm good. No, none of that would work. He played it safe, "HI ALICE. THANKS FOR REACHING OUT. IF WE CAN CHAT WHEN YOU'RE FREE THAT WOULD BE GREAT. LOTS GOING ON."

No response.

George came out of the house, "Let's do this." They got into his red Ford Mustang GT and George fired up the engine, peeling out of his driveway. The backend fishtailed until he got it under control. "Wooo!" he yelled.

They got onto the 5 Freeway heading North. "Hollywood, here we come," George said. "You ready, Freddy? This is your fucking day." George was pumped like a football jock before a big game. Freddy nodded and smiled.

George blasted his favorite band besides Wasting June, The Cars. "I fucking love the 80's." He started to sing *Shake It Up,* badly.

Freddy just laughed and looked out the window. He couldn't shake the random text from Alice Cooper. It had stirred something inside of him.

George lowered the volume, "Dude, what's up?"

Freddy looked at him, "Nothing. I'm excited."

George glanced at him while watching the road. He gave Freddy his look that said, "I don't believe you."

"Seriously," Freddy chuckled, "I'm fine." He slapped the armrest, "Let's do this!"

George smiled, turned up the volume. *"All I Want Is You"* came on next. George sang along once again. Lip syncing several of the slow spots getting Freddy to laugh out loud.

The song ended, and George turned off the tunes. "Okay, let's talk."

Freddy, surprised, said, "About?"

"Something's fucking eating you up. And the good friend that I am, I want to talk about it," George said in his matter-of-fact voice.

Freddy took a deep breath, leaned his head back, smiling, "Fuck."

"Well, that is a good start. More words, please."

Freddy looked at him, "You know I hate talking about me…"

"Yeah, that's your fucking problem. Now, I, on the other hand, love talking about me. But right now, we need to talk about what's going on inside that fucking head of yours. We have a two-hour drive so let's chat. Shall we?"

Freddy just laughed and then fell silent.

"Was it about that reporter at my party? I'm sorry, man, I didn't know who she was. She got in as a guest with a friend of mine. Don't worry, I laid into him good."

"No, it wasn't that at all."

"Then what the fuck is it? If you don't fucking talk, I will play country music all the way there."

"Okay, fine," Freddy put out his hands. "I'll talk. You're worse than a fucking terrorist."

"I'll take that as a compliment. Now, talk."

"So, I'm thinkin' about flying to Boise to get Jenny back."

"Really? What's your game plan there?"

"I don't know. She said I didn't fight for her, so I think if I just go out there and then see what happens—"

"Go out there? See what happens? Dude, no. You need to fight. You need to have a *Pretty Woman* fucking moment. *Jerry McGuire* kind of shit. Come up with a speech."

"A speech?"

"Yeah, at least prepare and then adapt to the situation. I go into business deals just the same. I've got my plan, I've got my non-negotiables, and then I've got to adapt to whatever the opposing side's demands are."

"So, I need to treat Jenny like a business deal?"

"Exactly, you need to get in there and mean some serious fucking business, dude. Chicks love that. It's manly. It gets them all hot and shit."

Freddy was thinking about it.

George said, "See, you are thinking about it right now, and that is your fucking problem. You think too much."

Freddy thought some more.

George laughed, "You're thinking about everything I fucking say, dude. Okay, so do you know what she wants besides fighting for her?"

"She wants me to keep going to a shrink."

"That's it?"

"Yeah."

"Dude, done and done. No brainer." George paused, "Oh, wait, no, this fucking guy next to me does have a brain. What's the big fucking deal about going to a shrink?"

"I don't know. I just…"

"Just what? She gave you her non-negotiable, and you countered with," his voice went low, "umm, umm, I don't know. Let me think about it."

Freddy got animated, "I just want to go back to normal, is all. And shrinks aren't normal."

There was silence.

George said, "Okay, so you want normal, but I think what you need to realize is that there is no normal, dude. Some fucked up unbelievable shit happened in your life, and it's never gonna be normal. This is where we adapt. Life is one big fucking business deal. Life has some non-negotiables, and we need to adapt."

There was silence.

George took a deep breath, "Let's get through tonight. Have some fun. Don't think about any of this shit. Then let's reset tomorrow with a game plan. I'll work on it with you."

Freddy nodded, "Thanks." His cell phone rang.

George glanced down at the name. "Fuck, Alice Cooper is calling you?"

Freddy stared at the cell.

George said, "You gonna fucking answer that?"

Freddy continued to stare.

George snatched the phone from it, resting on his leg. Freddy wasn't fast enough to stop him. George answered it on speaker, "Hello?"

Alice Cooper's voice said, "Freddy?"

"Hey, Alice, this is George. Hold on. I'll get Freddy."

"Hey, George, what's up?"

"Nothing. Doing good. Livin the dream. Hold on."

George silently instructed Freddy to say something.

Freddy said, hesitation in his voice, "Hey, Alice."

"Freddy?"

"Yeah."

"Hey man, good to hear your voice. You said give you a call when I could chat. Is this a good time?"

Freddy didn't answer, but George mimicked Freddy's voice, "Yeah."

"Okay, good. So, lots going on, huh?"

George punched Freddy in the arm and raised his eyebrows in distress.

Freddy rubbed his arm and gave George a pissed off face. He then said, "Yeah, lots going on."

"Well, hey, listen, you popped up in my prayer time, and I thought I would text you and see how you're doing. So what's up?"

"Well, it's complicated."

"Shit, if I had a dollar for every time I heard that, then I'd be a rich man. Life is complicated."

"Well, you know about my daughter who was killed. My wife Jenny left me a year ago because we both couldn't deal with the loss together. I blame me. She blames herself. Anyway, she came back recently. And… and, well, I had a chance to get her back, and I fucked it up."

"Freddy," Alice started, "I've learned one thing over the years. Now, I'm no saint when it comes to women. I've had my issues. Women want to be loved. And us, guys, we want to be loved, but what we want the most is respect. This is where we mess it up. We work on respecting our women, and that's not what they want. They want to be loved. Love is action, my friend."

George nodded his head.

Freddy said, "Yeah, she said that I didn't fight for her."

"Love in action," Alice confirmed. "Listen, it's gonna be alright. Be humble. Let her know your process and let her know where you messed up. All you can do is own your shit and be you, fully alive. Make sense?"

"Yeah, it does. Thank you."

"You bet. Hey, I gotta go."

"Alice?"

"Yeah."

"That talk about the Narnia guy really affected me."

"Really? That's awesome. God is amazing. He has a knack for changing what we think is unchangeable."

"Yeah, I'm still navigating my feelings."

"Freddy, someone told me this once. I needed to hear it. They said, 'Alice, in order to navigate life, you need a compass.' I asked, 'Where do I get this compass?' He said, 'It's the Bible.' Freddy, get yourself one of them compasses and start in the Book of John. Be blessed, my friend, and we'll talk soon. Love ya."

"Alice, thank you."

"Take care." He hung up.

"WHAT THE FUUUCCCKKK? That was AWESOME!" George said. "Did he just say, I love you?"

Freddy smirked.

George said, "That was some good shit right there. Wow!" George grabbed Freddy's shirt on his arm and pushed him back and forth in excitement. Freddy's, skinny body, slammed into the car door back and forth. He let go, "Woooo! That was crazy fucking awesome!"

The adrenaline settled while George continued to hoot, holler. and talk about what happened. Freddy went into the recesses of his mind to contemplate all that was said. He thought, *"I need to love Jenny and stop expecting respect from her."*

Freddy whispered, "I need a compass."

George settled and said, "Yeah, a fucking compass. That was a good analogy." He paused, "Hey, where do we get it?"

Freddy simply said, "Amazon."

"Dude, are you ready for tonight. This is gonna be epic!"

Freddy looked straight ahead. His answer wasn't mechanical. It wasn't from the surface of regular conversation but instead from the depth of his soul. His answer wasn't about the event tonight. It was a future event with Jenny. "Yeah, I'm ready."

CHAPTER 27
HOLLYWOOD FOREVER CEMETERY

GEORGE PULLED IN and parked as they directed him. The place was packed. Once George gave the attendants his name, they VIP'd him all the way. Hollywood Forever Cemetery was located in the heart of Hollywood on Sunset Boulevard, directly behind the Paramount Pictures Studio. Hollywood Forever was a large, meticulously maintained cemetery with manicured landscapes, amazing gardens, and even a central lake. In addition, it was dotted with tall palms, beautiful flowers, and massive ornate mausoleums. Old Hollywood stars were buried in the cemetery; Mickey Rooney, Marilyn Monroe, George C. Scott, Cecil B. DeMille, and many more. They even had a statue in memory of Toto, the little dog from the Wizard of Oz. It was a sixty-two-acre paradise tucked within the nasty derelict section of Hollywood.

"What are you not telling me?" Freddy asked as he pointed to the sign in front of the car. It read, "George Casey."

"Well, I might have become a sponsor for tonight's little gathering," George smiled. "Just get the fuck out."

An attendant opened their doors and led them through the park past the thousands of people waiting to get inside. It was still daylight, 5:14 pm, but the sun was setting fast. Freddy saw people with blankets and chairs, pillows, games, ice chests, and whatnot, waiting to get frisked by the security guards at the gate. George and Freddy bypassed them all.

"George, should we have gotten the blankets and chairs from the car?" They had put everything in the trunk before they left.

"We'll come back for it."

Freddy had an inkling that they weren't going back to the car until the night was over. That thought was confirmed when the attendants took them to a private section of the grass to the left of the large field. It was closed off to the public with red velvet ropes latched through gold stanchions. Inside, a table awaited them, dressed with white linen topped with a tombstone centerpiece that dripped with blood-red flowers.

Freddy whistled when he saw the entire open field filled with people. The event was sold out. There would be over three-thousand patrons watching the movie. Surrounding the open field were grave-stones of Hollywood's elite mixed in amongst the average joes. Huge mausoleums decorated the background of the large white wall where they would project the movie. More palms dotted the skyline above the white stretch of wall where the movie would be projected onto.

"Happy birthday, dude," George swept his left arm out to the private table. "And we have our own VIP section with chairs and blankets in the front row for the movie."

Freddy said, "I guess we don't have to go back to the car." He looked at the table, the park, and then back to George, "Thank you. This means a lot."

Just then, they were rushed by several people. Freddy turned in surprise to see two co-workers and his boss, Bob. "What the hell?"

They yelled, "Surprise!"

Freddy looked at George, who was grinning and begging for Freddy to say his favorite line. "Just say it," George said.

In the background, a DJ played music. People were eating and drinking and socializing everywhere. Many were dressed in Freddy Krueger's iconic red and green sweater. Some wore Halloween masks and sported a plastic knock-off version of his bladed gloved hand.

The DJ interjected as he lowered the volume of the music, "Attention everyone, we have a special announcement in a few minutes before we start the F.K. Kill Counter. You have been warned." He flared the music volume up, drowning the applause.

George looked at Freddy, confused. Freddy answered the question he didn't verbalize, "Freddy Kreuger Kill Counter. It's something us die-hards like to do. Count all the kills in the movie."

"Ah, roger that."

They sat at the table. Wine and beer were served along with various appetizers.

The music faded again, and the DJ announced in a deep voice, drawing out each word, "Ladies and Gentlemen, those dead and alive, please welcome our host for this special nightmarish evening, the creator of Cinespia itself, John Wyatt."

The crowd went nuts. Freddy stood on his feet, applauding. So did his co-workers and boss. George stood out of obligation.

The forty-year-old man, brown hair, hipster dress, shouted into the mic, "Welcome everyone. Are you ready for Freddy?" The crowd yelled in response. "Well, first things first. I want to thank our sponsor for tonight's event. George Casey, CEO of Hang In There Gym and Sports." A spotlight hit George directly. He raised his hand in acknowledgment. The crowd applauded. "Go to his website, hang in there gym dot com. Now, we have a special movie for tonight." Several people screamed and hollered. "We are coming up to the 32nd anniversary of this beloved cult classic. Now, when Wes Craven brought this baby to life." Hundreds applauded the name of the director. "He had no idea that we would be here today in this most iconic location. A graveyard." Cheers erupted.

John continued to talk, but the crowd noticed someone sneaking up behind him. It was someone dressed in full Freddy Krueger costume. The make-up was to perfection—the hat and sweater spot on. The bladed glove looked real. The actor put up his bladed index finger, informing the crowd to *shhhhhh*. He approached the unsuspecting John Wyatt until he was right behind him.

The actor spoke in his own wired mic from somewhere within the costume, "I'm your boyfriend now, John." The place erupted in chaos as they cheered, whistled, clapped, and screamed.

Freddy looked at George, "That is fucking epic. He sounds just like him."

George smiled and nodded.

John Wyatt said, "Wow! Freddy, you're here."

"Where else would I rather be? I'm ready to enter everyone's dreams tonight."

John, on cue, said his cheesy line, "Sounds like a nightmare, to me."

The actor stared at him, menacingly, "Nightmares for some. Others...wet dreams!"

The crowd laughed.

The actor continued, "One wet dream in particular. Yes, someone that likes to go by my name. Freddy. After tonight he will want to change his name to Mommy."

The crowd laughed.

John asked, "Who is this Freddy, Freddy?"

The actor raised his clawed glove toward John, "Don't try to be funny, honey. You don't got what it takes." He turned back to the crowd, "This one goes by the name Freddy Foley."

George smacked Freddy's shoulder, "That's you, bud."

Freddy looked at George, "You've got to be fucking kidding me."

"I don't fucking joke, dude. Get up there."

The spotlight hit Freddy at the table. Thousands of eyes fixed on him.

The actor said, "Come up here, Freddy. I got something to say to you."

Freddy moved reluctantly at first, then picked up momentum. He stood next to the actor, who looked even more amazing up close. John Wyatt shook Freddy's hand and handed him the microphone.

The actor said, "So what do you think of my place?" He waved his arms to point out the cemetery they were in.

Freddy said, shyly into the mic, "I love it."

"Well, a man of few words." The crowd laughed. "And what do you do for work, Freddy? For example, I kill people." The crowd laughed again.

Freddy answered, "I embalm people."

This garnered much surprise from the onlookers, including the actor.

"Well," the actor said, "it will be hard to embalm what I leave behind." The crowd laughed. "Tell me, Embalmer, what are you dreaming about?"

Freddy was taken back by the question. He looked around embarrassed, not knowing what to say or how to respond.

The actor pressured him, "Do you not have a dream? Perhaps a nightmare," he growled. The crowd cheered. "What about a special someone in your life, Freddy? Have any of those types of dreams?" The crowd laughed at the not-so-subtle joke.

Freddy raised the mic, "Actually, yeah, I do. I dream to be with someone, someone special."

"Oh, how nice. Is that special someone here? Is it me?" The crowd laughed.

"No, she's not here. I wish she were."

A few of the ladies were ahh'd by his confession. Placing hands over their hearts.

"And why is this special someone not here with you on this special night all about me?" More laughs.

"Well, Mr. Krueger, this is kind of awkward." Hundreds chuckled. "I don't know." He paused, "Wait, I do know. It was because I'm an asshole." Many cheered at his admittance.

The actor said, "Well, we all knew you were an asshole." They laughed. "We are going to play a little game this evening. You like games, right, Freddy?"

"Not really."

"Good." Crowd laughed. "Bring them in."

Freddy turned to see three other Freddy Krueger's in full costume walk out and stand to the left of the audience.

The actor said, "One of these Freddy's will be your date this evening." The crowd cheered at the realization of what was going on. "I call it Welcome to My World, Bitch!" The crowd erupted with cheers and laughter at one of Freddy Kreuger's best one-liners known by his followers.

Freddy was laughing. The actor said, "Do you find this funny?"

He nodded as he laughed. Freddy pointed at his best friend and George smiled, pointing back.

"So, this is how it works. Each one of them will say three phrases. Based on their phrases, you will choose one of them to be your date for the evening to watch my movie. Understood?"

Freddy laughed and nodded in agreement.

"Great, let the one-liners begin. Our first contestant is tall, has a very tan complexion, and loves to wear comfortable clothes while stalking teenage boys who wet their beds."

The Krueger on the far left stepped forward. These actors didn't walk with confidence and were fidgety with the microphone. "When at school, I don't run in the hallway." The voice was female. She sounded older, and the line she said was flat and stale. The crowd chuckled out of sympathy because they recognized another Freddy one-liner, 'no running in the hallway,' in his movie just before killing someone. But this contestant said they don't run in the hallway. It was definitely awkward. Several booed.

She said the next phrase, "Now I'm playing with power." The line was delivered flat, and the crowd let her know it with more boo's. Someone yelled out, "NEXT!" Laughter ensued.

Freddy said into the mic, "C'mon, give her a chance." More of the ladies in the crowd ooo'd and ahhh'd.

She said the final phrase more embarrassed than ever. You could tell she wanted to leave, but she delivered the last line. "You look tired. Have a seat." That was exactly what the crowd yelled back. "Have a seat!" She stepped back in line. The Krueger in the middle stepped forward.

A male voice said, "Why are you screaming? I haven't even cut you yet." The crowd erupted not because of the rapid delivery of the line but because it was a man.

The second line, "You've got nothing to worry about. This won't hurt a bit." And then the last line quickly came after this, "You can check-in, but you can't check out." Then he stepped back in line with the other two costumed contestants. The crowd clapped for the fun of it. Some boo'd. Some said, "Hell yeah, pick that one."

The main actor said to Freddy, "So, have you made a decision yet. Should we skip the third? You look intrigued by number two." The crowd laughed and cheered.

Freddy responded, "No, let's hear the last one."

"Oh, an equal opportunist, are we?" More laughs.

The third stepped forward. It was a female voice, and the first line was, "Wanna suck face?" She stuck out her tongue through the mask. The crowd cheered.

The main actor responded, "Oh, we have a live one here."

She delivered her second line, "I'm your girlfriend now, bitch." Thunderous yelling and applause sounded.

"And what is your last line before Freddy here chooses?" The actor asked.

She said the last line, "Every sunset is a new painting."

The crowd went silent. That wasn't any one-liner Freddy Krueger had ever said in any of his movies. Freddy watched as this third mystery contestant pulled the hat and mask away from her face.

He coughed out, "Jenny?"

She ran into his arms and kissed him.

The actor said, "We have a winner, and they are definitely sucking face."

Freddy and Jenny blocked everyone out of their mind. It was just them. The thousands blurred in the background.

The actor tapped Freddy on the shoulder, "Am I interrupting?" They pulled apart smiling and half-embarrassed as thousands watched them make-out. The actor continued, "I have a confession." He turned to the audience and then took off his hat, throwing it into the crowd. He then proceeded to peel away the prosthetic make-up from his face. Someone in the crowd yelled, "Holy shit, it's Robert Englund!" He was correct. It was the actor who played the legendary Freddy Krueger. The crowd went ballistic. He waved to everyone and bowed. He shook Freddy and Jenny's hands, thanking them for being part of the intro. He then went back to the crowd with the microphone in hand. "I want to thank you all for coming tonight. Please give a big hand to John Wyatt, founder of Cinespia." He waited for the clapping to settle. "We want to thank tonight's sponsor, George Casey, of Hang In There Gym and Sports." More claps ensued.

John Wyatt said, "And let's give a shout out to Robert Englund, ladies and gentlemen." Robert waved and bowed to the cheering audience, who stood on their feet in appreciation.

"Enjoy the show, everyone!"

Freddy and Jenny walked back to the table where George and the others stood applauding. The two other contestants followed them. George pointed for Freddy to look behind him. He turned and watched both contestants pull away their masks to reveal Jenny's parents. He was shocked. They all hugged. Everyone at the table began to mix and mingle with hello's and intros.

Freddy sidled up next to George in awe, "I can't even...I don't know..." He was flabbergasted.

George gave a big grin, leaned back a bit with hands half-raised, "Just admit it. You know the words."

Freddy said, shock still registering on his face, "You are truly a fucking giver."

"That's my boy!" George grabbed him in a big hug. "Happy birthday, my friend."

CHAPTER 28
I DON'T BELIEVE IT

"I STILL DON'T BELIEVE it," Freddy said as he pulled Jenny in close. "You're actually here." The movie started, but they had walked out into the darkness and stood in front of a lit mausoleum.

"Here I am. In the flesh." She kissed him.

They pulled away. Their eyes locked together. Freddy said with all sincerity, "I'm sorry, Jenny. Truly, I am. I was an asshole."

"You definitely were an asshole. But I'm sorry as well. We both have to process this together, and it's gonna be tough. We can't run away from it."

"You're right. And I want you to know that I was going to fly out and see you."

"George didn't want to wait for you, so he called me and set this entire thing up in September." She hesitated, "I told him no at first, but he still bought the tickets, flight, everything." She added, "How much money does he really have?"

"I don't know, but driving up here, he was wondering how much it cost to be buried at this cemetery. I told him half-a-million. He didn't blink."

They sat on the steps of the unknown grave holding hands.

Freddy said, "Listen, I will do whatever it takes, Jenny. Therapist every week, every day, every second, hell, I will have them move in with me."

She laughed and squeezed his arm as she leaned in. "I love you, Freddy Foley. Always have. Always will."

They held each other for several minutes. In the background, they could hear the movie playing and the die-hard crowd reacting.

Freddy finally said, "I can't believe your parents actually did that. Dressing up and going out there like that."

She pulled back, "I know, right? They didn't even know the movie." She paused, "They did it for you. They did it for us."

He looked down at the ground, "I know." He looked up at her and smiled, "They're awesome."

She said, "I can't believe George got them to do it. He set it all up, by the way."

"I figured the mastermind was involved but had no idea."

"Yeah, he contacted Robert Englund's agent and the founder of this thing, then sponsored the entire event."

"That's crazy."

They leaned into each other, and Freddy put his arm around her waist. Several minutes went by.

"Jenny?"

"Yeah."

"I met this dude who told me about the guy who wrote Narnia."

"C.S. Lewis?"

"Yeah, I think so."

"Who was this guy that told you about him?"

"Alice Cooper."

She pulled away and looked at his face to see if he was telling the truth.

He put his hands up in surrender. "Honest."

"Your nostrils aren't flaring," she said. This was his tell-tale sign for telling a lie. "Let me guess...George."

"Yeah, kind of in a way. We got to meet Alice Cooper backstage, and then when he found out I was an embalmer, he invited me to meet him in his hotel room the next morning to talk."

"And he randomly brought up Lewis?"

"I don't remember all the details of how we got there, but he started talking religion."

"Uh-oh," she responded. "I hope you didn't come on too strong with him."

"No, I was a gentleman about it. But I did voice my opinion. He basically said life is a pursuit of truth. The Narnia guy apparently was an atheist."

"Really?" she said.

"Yeah, one day he went to the zoo, and he said before he left he was not a believer, but when he got there, he was. I know it sounds strange, but it kind of happened to me."

She looked puzzled, "What happened?"

"When I got on the plane, I didn't believe, but when I got off the plane, I did. I don't understand it."

"So, what, you're a Christian?"

"No...I don't know...maybe. Don't you have to go to church to be a Christian?"

She giggled, "I don't think it works like that, dear."

He laughed and then started tickling her, "Oh, and you know how it works?"

She screamed and laughed, fending off Freddy's probing hands. Hands that began to be more adventurous. Hands she had missed. They passionately kissed.

Freddy slowly pulled away and whispered, "I love you, Jenny Foley."

She whispered back, "I love you, Freddy Foley."

He fell to one knee and produced a diamond ring, "Will you marry me, again?"

Complete shock hit her face. Her hands covered her mouth as her blue eyes quickly glassed over. Her left hand slowly descended down, shaking. "Yes...yes, I will." He placed the ring on her finger. It was the same wedding ring she had worn for seven years.

Freddy pulled themselves to their feet, and they kissed again. He began to pull her to the side of the beige-colored stone mausoleum. "Where are you taking me?" she playfully asked between kisses.

Freddy didn't answer. He didn't have to. She went willingly. They made love behind the grave in the green grass.

When they finished, they stared up at the stars. She rested her head on his arm, tucked behind her head.

Something suddenly dawned on her, "Wait, you had the ring with you, but you didn't know I was going to be here."

Freddy smiled and said a single word, "George."

"But how?" she faltered.

He kissed her. Her eyes still open in puzzlement, but she kissed him back. They pulled away.

"George handed it to me at the table. He brought it. He didn't know but planned for the best. I had given him the ring to hold onto. To keep it safe."

Her face lit up in astonishment. "He's a keeper."

They laughed, kissed, and made love again under the stars in a graveyard while *A Nightmare on Elm Street* played in the distance.

Freddy thought, *"Dreams do come true. And the best part? Jenny is mine."*

CHAPTER 29
THIS WORLD FAILED YOU

THE PARK WAS very familiar to Steven Murdock. Two days away from Halloween. He watched the children chase each other, swing on the monkey bars, climb, and play. The sounds of their laughter, a foreign sound in his early years. His childhood had been ripped away—no joy to be found in his life. It was snuffed out, right from the beginning. Now his joy was doing god's bidding and seeing angels born.

There she was, the one his god had told him about. She played alone quietly near the playground. Steven watched her look at the other kids zooming around her. She was skinny with brown, scraggly hair, wearing a plain pink dress with smudges of dirt on it.

"Homely," Steven thought, *"This world failed you, my darling. A great gift comes to you."* His special trash bag was waiting in the bathroom. He cleaned the area. Always watching. Always ready. He felt a tinge of pain enter his chest but shrugged it off. Though his discomfort showed on his face, Steven continued to clean the drinking fountain while maintaining visual contact with the little girl.

It was time. She got up and walked toward the bathroom. Steven had the maintenance sign ready as she walked by him. Zombie-like, pale, emotionless. She stepped inside. Steven moved quickly, placing the A-frame yellow sign in front. Another girl rushed to go in, but he held out his hand, "Come back later." She back peddled away in surprise and then skipped away in confusion.

Steven went inside the bathroom. The girl was on the ground convulsing. She was having a seizure. "No," he said. "She's not the one. She is tainted." He lifted her up, cradling her, and kicked the front door open. A couple walking by gasped. Steven called out, "Call 9-1-1!" Others heard, and the murmuring intensified. Several people were calling.

Steven placed her convulsing body in the grass. Parents and children began to gather. He turned her to her side in case she vomited. Steven opened her mouth to inspect that the tongue was not obstructing her breathing. He sat there and sighed while looking at all the faces. Cell phone cameras watched the event unfold.

A woman screamed, "Sara! Oh, my God! Sara!" The mother went to her daughter's side. Others who had witnessed the event told her that the maintenance guy saved her.

Steven felt weak. Beads of sweat began to accumulate on his forehead. He couldn't breathe. The people around him spun and his eyes crossed. He felt numbness take hold of his left arm—his heart racing—struggling. He was thirsty. His mouth was dry.

"Water," he struggled.

No one heard him over the screams and crying of the mother and those calling 911. No one came to Steven's rescue. Some patted him on the shoulder to thank him for saving the girl. His eyes blurred in and out. In slow motion, he fell over to his side. Steven saw the face of the little girl and his eyes fixed on hers. Her seizure had stopped. Drool ran from her mouth. She was coherent, staring at Steven. There was the slightest lift of her open mouth—an attempted smile. Steven couldn't return his own smile even though he longed to do so. His smiles were stolen at her age. Everything suddenly seized inside of him. The world went black.

CHAPTER 30
THE TEXT MESSAGE

OST PEOPLE DISLIKE Mondays, but Freddy Foley didn't mind them. The only time he didn't like them was when he nursed a hangover after a night with George. Though it was a rare occasion to be partying on Sunday night, the exception would be October 30th when you have a Halloween party till three in the morning. George always looked for any excuse to have a party. Halloween was one reason, but the main point of having a party Sunday night was the fact that Freddy's official birthday was October 31st. At midnight, the party truly began.

Freddy, wearing sunglasses to cover his exhausted eyes, exited his car. It was Monday, October 31st—his official thirty-fifth birthday. He slept most of the day. Halloween was an official holiday at his company. It was a day most in his line of work celebrated. Freddy however, loved to work. It was quiet, devoid of co-workers, and there were plenty of decedents to embalm. It was a long weekend, and even though his hangover lingered, he was excited to get back to work. He was even more excited about Jenny coming home from Idaho in a couple of weeks. With every day that passed, he missed her more and more.

The sun was setting. He checked his cell. 5:57 pm. One missed text message. He opened it. It was from Alice Cooper. It read, HEY FREDDY. THOUGHT YOUD LIKE THIS. CRAZY! Attached was a YouTube video link. Freddy closed it to wait until he got back in his office to review the video. Freddy thought, *"Great, I hope I don't have a rock legend texting me annoying videos to watch."*

He punched in his access code at the back entrance. The green light flashed on and the door unlocked. He entered the kitchen and made his way to his office.

Opening his office, he was overwhelmed by black balloons, black roses, and a poster-sized cardboard congratulations sign with happy birthday messages from the Pinewood family. He smiled and said, "Awe, thanks, team. You guys warm my cold heart." He chuckled.

Freddy sat in his office chair and noticed a sealed envelope with the Pinewood logo stamp on his desk. It didn't look like a birthday card. Freddy opened it. As he read the letter, his heart pounded in excitement. He grabbed his phone, took a picture, then texted it to Jenny and George.

HOLY SHIT! IM IN TOP 10 FOR EMBALMER OF THE YEAR!

He looked at the letter with a mix of unbelief and joy. Jenny texted back that she was proud of him. George followed with IT WASNT ME THIS TIME. ALL YOU BRO. CONGRATS. LETS PARTY LOL. Freddy paled at the thought of partying and said under his breath, "No fucking way."

He looked at the chart of decedents that had come in over the weekend and the schedule for each. "Well, time to get to work."

He stood and walked into the embalming room. He proceeded to get things ready, instruments cleaned, fluids prepared. As he walked to get his first body, another text message chimed in. It was Alice Cooper. DID YOU WATCH IT.

Freddy replied out loud as he opened the door, "No, Alice, not yet. Working, dude."

Another follow up message came in. WATCH IT NOW. LET ME KNOW WHAT YOU THINK. EVER THOUGHT OF TRYING IT.

Freddy, puzzled by the last statement, decided to play the video. He clicked the link. The YouTube app opened, and the video began to play. He noticed it was titled "Cockroach Life and Death."

The camera was close up to a man holding an upside-down dead cockroach in the palm of his hand.

"Okay, everyone, we just got out of a powerful teaching about raising the dead. I'm in my apartment with my brother in the Lord, and we decided to do some practicing. We found this dead cockroach in the closet and said what the heck let's try this." The camera bobbled around as the man talking touched the cockroach. There was a hollow crunchy sound. He flicked it in his hand, trying to get it to move, but it was lifeless. Legs didn't move. Antennae were still. "Okay, so the cockroach is confirmed to be dead. I'm Bryan, and this is Steve. He moved the camera to see both of their faces. They were normal looking in all regards. Groomed hair, however, one needed a haircut. Bryan wore glasses. "Say hi, Steve."

"Hi." he waved.

The camera jostled as it focused back on the dead cockroach. He touched it again. It sounded flaky, like touching a stale potato chip. Bryan said, "Okay, so if we as believers read scripture that says we can raise the dead, then why not practice. Steve, why don't you read the scripture."

"Okay," there was the sound of thin paper turning in the background. "It reads in Matthew ten, verse eight, 'Heal the sick, raise the dead, cleanse those who have leprosy, drive out demons. Freely you have received; freely give'."

Bryan spoke, "Okay, so there you have it. God says we should go out into the world and do these things in His name as believers. We are going to pray for this cockroach to be raised back from the dead."

The camera wobbled a bit but stayed focused on the cockroach in the palm of his hand. It was still on its back, not moving. Steve's hand came into the picture like he was going to cast a spell over the insect.

Steve prayed, "Fire of God. Raise this cockroach back to life in Jesus' name. We call fire of life down from heaven."

Bryan jumped in, "Yes, Father God, we speak life over it. Come back to life in Jesus' name."

Nothing happened.

They doubled their efforts, both speaking in a strange language he had never heard before. It sounded like a mixture of French and German, but nothing Freddy could make out. It was gibberish. English words were inserted like 'fire of God' or 'Jesus'.

The volume of the two men increased. They spoke with passion and conviction. Nothing happened.

The men began to laugh and giggle. The camera jostled for a second but remained on the cockroach. He thought they gave up. Freddy almost stopped watching the video when suddenly.

Bryan yelled, "LIFE! In Jesus' name!"

The cockroach's legs began to wiggle. Antennae stirred. It popped out of the man's hand. The camera followed the once dead insect as it scurried around the linoleum floor. Bryan and Steve were screaming. One of them lifted his leg high, stomped on the ground, crushing the cockroach. The video went blank and ended.

Freddy was stunned. He whispered mechanically, "What the fuck?"

He scrolled down to read comments left by thousands.

"I can't believe you killed it," one read.

"OMG, You killed it!" another read.

Message after message was about the cockroach being killed. Others argued that they couldn't believe it came back to life.

One message stood out to Freddy the most, "Everyone WTF, why are you so bothered that they killed a cockroach. I don't care if it was raised back to life. It's still an effing cockroach."

Freddy closed the app on his phone and looked up at the cadavers lined up in front of him. Each laying on their individual carts.

"They did it," he said. "They raised it back to life. It fucking worked."

CHAPTER 31
HOW ABOUT YOU, HERO?

S TILL BLOWN AWAY by what he had just seen, Freddy grabbed the chart of his first decedent. The chart dangled from the stainless-steel cart. "Steven Murdock, age forty-nine, wow, young, Mr. Murdock. Ah, died of heart failure." Freddy sighed, "Sorry about your broken heart, Mr. Murdock. I'm Freddy Foley and will be your caretaker this evening. I'm gonna bring you to the finish line, my friend."

He continued to read the chart. "Fully paid. Burial plot #1127. Northwest view. Type: Standard." Freddy raised his eyebrows, "Good job, Mr. Murdock. You already had everything lined up." He continued to read, "Let's see, no service. No service? Mr. Murdock, do you not have any family or friends?" He sighed again, "Well, I will see what I can do for you. Okay, blah, blah, blah, technical jargon. Ah, this is interesting, says here you died a hero saving a little girl. Wow, a hero. *And* saving a little girl."

Freddy checked his vitals first. Dead. Then he logged the facial features and made marks next to each line item on his list. Brown hair, shaved face, pudgy cheeks, no abnormalities. "Okay, Mr. Murdock, I'm just getting acquainted with your face and structure of your body; seeing if there will be any extra challenges I might have before we start the process. It's all formality, but everything looks in good order." Freddy paused and took a good look at Steven Murdock. He said quietly, "I wish you were around to save my little-girl, Mr. Murdock." He stared at him for a long moment, then snapped back to work, "Alright, let's get you prepped and ready."

He unlocked the wheels and pushed the body of Steven Murdock down the hall to the embalming room. He positioned him in stall number one, tilted the body down at a slight angle, allowing the water and fluids to run down the sides to the bottom trough drain. He placed a block pillow under his head, "Here ya go, Mr. Murdock. A little comfort."

Freddy suited up with his Personal Protective Equipment, then sat in the stainless-steel chair nearby and rolled to the counter. He filled out the necessary paperwork. His mind kept creeping back to the memory of the two guys raising the cockroach back to life. He pulled his cell out of his pocket and watched the video again. He paused it when the cockroach came to life and jumped from his hand. It was in mid-air. He stared at the screenshot for a long time.

Memories of the talk-radio guy came to his mind. *Faith in normal people like you and me raising others back from the dead.* Then words from Alice Cooper. *All truths are not the same. It's up to us as humans to find the ultimate truth—the truth above all truths.*

Two words bombarded his mind; Truth and Faith; Faith and Truth. The little girl he tried to raise flashed in his mind. He saw his daughter calling out to him to help her. The failure of it bolted back into his consciousness. His heart raced. He could feel it beating inside his chest. "No, Freddy, not again," he whispered. "You're not going to fuck this up. It's you and Jenny now. The past is the past. Move on, you stupid idiot."

He turned to his patient and rolled his chair over to him, "Sorry to keep you waiting, Mr. Murdock. I'm gonna wash your body and get you all cleaned up. Sound good? Alright, let's do this."

Freddy spent the next several minutes washing Steven Murdock. He noticed the many welts on his inner thighs. Some scarred, others freshly scabbed. "What happened here, Mr. Murdock? I'm no detective, but they look self-inflicted. It's okay, I won't tell anyone. Our little secret. No one will ever see them." Freddy massaged the muscles. Lifting up layers of fat to focus the water while rubbing soap with his gloved hand. Dirty water rolled down the sides of the embalming table and sloshed down the drain. Water splashed and sprayed into his face shield. The hollow sound of the running water hitting against the flesh soothed Freddy, but he found himself thinking about what was possible and what was impossible. His mind descended further away from his work. Deep down inside, he believed that supernatural things could occur. Even deeper than that, in thoughts not even thought about. Thoughts buried in the hidden recesses of sub-molecular levels itself bubbled to the surface like molten lava coming alive. Even the absurd fictitious character of Freddy Krueger crept out. It wasn't the character but the sensation of a movie describing a regular man coming back from the grave. All these reflections and visions bounced inside his imagination. It was like frantically playing a pinball game with only one hand. Somewhere inside of him, he believed it possible that what was once dead could come back alive again. He longed for it to be real. He envisioned Mr. Murdock coming alive. His eyes opening. Coughing as air filled his lungs. But only one question mattered to him if someone came back to this world, "What is out there? What is beyond this place?"

The water suddenly splashed onto his face shield and startled him. He snapped back and realized a lot of the water had flooded the floor and not made it into the sink. The emergency floor drain gurgled as it tried to receive it.

It was unlike Freddy not to be focused on his work. He looked back at his cell phone on the counter. It was a black screen. He visualized the cockroach, once dead, now alive. He slowly looked back at Mr. Murdock, once alive, now dead.

"Is it possible?" he thought. His eyes had not deceived him. The cockroach was dead. They prayed. It came back to life.

Freddy turned the water off. He spoke to his patient, "What about you, hero? Do you want to live?"

He laid his hand on Steven Murdock's chest. He took a deep breath, exhaled. Lifting his hand away in doubt, he stepped back. "What are you doing?" Freddy looked around the room just to make sure no one was watching. There were no video cameras in the embalming room for privacy reasons. "What the fuck are you doing, Freddy?" he said aloud. He snapped the wet gloves he had on off and then retrieved a new pair. As he walked back to the table, placing the new gloves on, he recalled how he had failed to raise the girl back to life. He picked up the chart again to review it. He had to get his mind back on his work. Freddy's eyes gravitated to the text about Steven dying a hero for saving a little girl. People would forever see Steven Murdock as that hero, not the depressed, self-harming, wounded man who died alone without family, but instead a hero. Steven didn't save her for the glory of fame. He did it because it was the right thing to do. He didn't need an audience of approval but instead the conviction of his heart to act.

Freddy slowly placed his gloved hand back onto the chest. He looked up toward the ceiling and said, "I don't really know you well, God. I don't really pray or know how to, but I'm gonna try." Freddy looked down at Steven Murdock. "This man died a hero saving someone else. I don't know why you wanted to take him now, but I ask on his behalf that you bring this man, Steven Murdock, back to life. Let him live again, Jesus, like you did with the little girl who was sleeping." Freddy waited, but nothing happened. He bent a little lower to speak into Steven's ear, "It's time to wake up, Mr. Murdock." Nothing happened. He sighed and then flippantly said, "Just get up and walk in Jesus' name."

Again, nothing happened. At first. Freddy turned away to get back to work, but he heard vibrations behind him. He turned to look and saw the body begin to shake. It was small shakes at first. Then it increased until Steven Murdock began violently convulsing to the point that his two-hundred and eighty-pound body lifted completely off the table. Freddy backed away. Mouth agape. Eyes wide.

Steam began to rise from the body.

"Holy shit." Freddy froze in amazement, which turned to fear as he backed himself to the wall.

The white steam turned yellow-hued. Freddy smelled smoke that changed to wretched sulfur. Distant screams resounded within the room like they came out of a dark tunnel. After a moment, the body stopped vibrating and settled. Steven's chest rose up and down in heaves. The smoke dissipated, but the smell lingered. His eyes shot open, and he sat upright, gasping for air.

"Holy shit," Freddy said under his breath.

Steven looked down at his naked body and began to shout, "I'm on fire! On fire! Fire!"

Freddy rushed to his side, hands out. "It's...it's alright. You're... you're safe." Freddy quickly pulled away when he saw what looked like flames under Steven's skin. "What the..." A glow he had not seen before in the chaos.

"FIRE!" Steven, wide-eyed, scared out of his mind, tried to push Freddy away. The table tipped to one side, and Steven tumbled to the floor with a loud crash. Adrenaline blocked the pain from the fall. He continued to scoot away, bumping into the chair. Finally, his back hit the far wall. Steven pulled his knees to his chest and trembled. Calculating each step, slowing his pace, Freddy made his way toward him. His hands were out as he tried to placate the risen cadaver.

Freddy's words were mechanical, but inside he was freaking out. As he said words aloud, all he could think was, *"Oh my fucking, God. You're back from the dead. This isn't fucking real. What the fuck is happening?"* but instead of those words, he said, "You're alright. You're at Pinewood Mortuary. My name's Freddy."

Steven's jaw quivered, "It's true." Tears began to well up. "It's all true." He cried.

Freddy took a few more steps closer. "It's okay. It's alright." Inside, Freddy continued to think, *"What the fuck just happened? I'm talking to a dead-man. I've lost my mind. I'm gonna lose Jenny."*

Freddy scampered to get an embalming apron then scuttled back to drape it over Steven. Steven clutched at the thin, plastic, aqua-green colored material. Freddy continued to smell the sulfur in the air, although the smoke had dissipated.

"Do you know who you are?"

The former dead-man clenched tighter to the apron, continuing to cry.

This wasn't in any of his school academics—How To Interact With A Decedent Who Comes Back To Life. Freddy asked again, "Do you know who you are? I need you to answer me."

Through tears, he croaked, "Steven."

"Okay, that's good. Yes, your name is Steven. Steven Murdock. Okay, so…" he looked around and spotted the toppled chair. He lifted it back up and sat in the chair. "Okay, so I'm sitting down. Let's walk through what just happened," Freddy said this more for himself at this point. He needed to process.

Steven began to settle. Tears still flowed.

Freddy said under his breath, "This is insane."

Steven said, "Am I? Am...am I?"

Freddy waited, but he couldn't find the word. "Are you what?" He tried to coach him.

"Am...am I...mental?"

Freddy scrunched his face, not knowing how to answer this. "Mental?" he questioned.

"Am...am I...in an asylum?"

"Oh, asylum. No, no, it's not like that. You're at a mortuary, Pinewood, in Oceanside, California. Do you remember what happened? To you, I mean."

"There was fire. It...was everywhere."

"Okay, what do you remember before the fire?" Freddy didn't see any burns on his body and knew he didn't die from a fire. He died of heart failure. The man had a heart attack.

Steven struggled to remember as he tried to figure out what was happening to him. "I can't remember," he said, out of breath and agitated.

"It's alright, it's alright, Steven." He held out his hands. "Um, okay, so I'm an embalmer. You are at a mortuary where you were going to be embalmed. You died two days ago from heart failure. Do you understand?"

Steven drifted in thought. Freddy said with emphasis, "Steven, do you understand?"

Lips quivering, "Ye, ye, yes."

"Are you cold? Of course, you're cold. I'll be right back with your clothes." Freddy slowly got up, holding one hand out to try and keep Steven calm. Freddy left the room and quickly went to storage to grab his burial clothes from the plastic bag with Steven Murdock's name on it.

When he got back to the embalming room, he noticed that Steven hadn't moved. He was still curled up against the wall with the apron over his scrunched-up knees. Only his face was visible. Shivering.

Freddy held out the bag. "Steven, here are the clothes you had pre-arranged to be buried in. Okay?" He slowly handed it to him. Steven lowered the apron and took it. He unzipped the plastic bag and pulled out a new pair of Dickies pants and his old work shirt from the city. It was stained. Steven Murdock's name stitched on the breast above the pocket. He stood and began to put the pants and shirt on. He didn't put the socks and shoes on, but he pulled out the belt. An old leather belt. Steven hesitated to put it on. He slowly lifted the belt to his nose and smelled it. Then inspected it like an old memento he hadn't seen in decades. It clearly meant something to him.

Freddy reached to help him with the belt, but Steven lurched away. Freddy backed up, hands out, "Sorry, it's alright. I...I just wanted to help." Steven settled. Freddy said, "Hey, listen, I can get you something from the fridge. Are you hungry?"

Freddy waited, but there was no response. "You're probably hungry. Let's sit down and eat something. Alright?"

Steven nodded.

"Okay, then. So the kitchen is this way. Just follow me." Freddy thought, *I'm fucking going insane. I'm having a dead-man follow me to the kitchen to eat something.*"

Steven followed but hesitated to leave the room.

"It's alright." Freddy stopped himself, "No, it's not alright. This is fucking insane. You were dead. Now we are talking." Steven was staring at him. Freddy said, "Say something, anything."

Somberness in his voice, Steven replied, "It's real. I *was* dead."

"This is fucking crazy." Freddy could see that Steven was scared. "I'm scared too, bro. But no one's here. It's just us. C'mon, follow me."

Steven looked down the half-lit hallway to his right and then straight ahead. No one was there. It was quiet. "C'mon," Freddy coached. "Just through this door." Freddy went to the door and opened it, holding it open. Beyond him was the kitchen.

Each step brought Steven Murdock more confidence in where he now was. His bare feet slid on the tiled floor as he clutched onto the leather belt with both hands against his chest. It was like a security blanket.

He finally made it to the entryway of the kitchen. Lights had automatically engaged when Freddy stepped in. The room had a single square table with four chairs. A refrigerator, microwave, and Keurig lined the far left side while the remaining storage cabinets lined two other sides. The room looked vaguely like an insane asylum with its creepy black and white checkered flooring, white cabinets, and a badly dented fridge door. The microwave light flickered eerily in the background.

"This is the employee kitchen, Steven. Let's sit down here," Freddy said. He pulled out a chair for Steven to sit, going to the other side to sit in a chair opposite. Steven crept into the room after looking around and slid into the white plastic chair.

Freddy stood up, saying, "Alright, let me see what we've got to eat." He went to the fridge and opened it. The soft inside light came on as he bent down to look at the shelves. The odor of something rotting inside forced him to pull away. He saw a couple of yogurt cups and grabbed them, then he snatched two white plastic spoons from the drawer nearby.

"Alright, nothing but the best for ya here, Steven." He pulled the top off and slid it over to Steven, spearing the spoon into his own pink yogurt. Steven stared at it, not moving. He still clutched the belt to his chest.

Freddy reached for the belt, "Hey, let's set that down and—"

Steven instantly pulled away, stood, and yelled, "NO!"

Freddy froze. He slowly sat back down. "Alright. No problem. I won't touch the belt. C'mon, sit down. Have some gourmet yogurt."

Steven relaxed again and sat back down. He didn't eat.

Freddy took one scoop and put it into his mouth. The plastic spoon echoed off his teeth as he scraped the contents into his closed mouth, pulling it out. He stabbed his yogurt. "Alright, Steven, let's talk. What happened?"

CHAPTER 32
FACING THE TRUTH

"I T'S ALL TRUE," Steven plainly said.

"What's true?"

He looked at Freddy hard, "Hell and Heaven. It's all true."

Freddy wasn't expecting that. "You were there? In both."

"No, hell. I was in hell." Steven's eyes drifted into memories. "Hideous, gruesome, unbelievable horror. The smell—death, and..." his voice trailed to silence.

"Steven, and what?"

"And pain! So much pain! I was skinned alive over and over and over! They bathed in my blood." His voice began to crack, emotion taking over.

"But you came back, Steven. You're here."

"Where is here? It's just..."

Freddy was so curious, "Just what?"

"It's an in-between. This world is a stop-over."

"To what?"

"Are you listening?" Steven's voice escalated, "To hell or to heaven! It's all true. All of it."

Freddy was interviewing someone who claimed firsthand

knowledge. Knowledge of what or if there was something after death. Steven began to cry. "It's alright," Freddy consoled, not really knowing how to be there for someone who had just been in the depths of hell. "You're safe now."

Steven's cry shifted to laughing, "Safe?" he said. He began to cry again, "I can't go back. I can't..."

"It's gonna be alright, Steven. We'll figure it out."

Steven's voice softened. His eyes looked through Freddy, "It's already figured out."

Freddy felt shivers up his spine. Steven stopped looking through Freddy and his eyes focused on him. "Let's, let's start from the beginning. Before you died, Steven, at the park. You rescued a little girl. Tell me what happened."

Steven's eyes rolled behind his lids halfway as his mind recalled the event. "Her eyes," he started. "Her eyes stared at me. Lying on the grass together."

None of it made sense to Freddy, but he coached him to tell more, "Okay, that's good. Lying on the grass with the little girl or someone else?"

Ignoring his question, "She wasn't the one. They had to be pure. She was sick."

"Yes, she was sick, and you saved her."

"She was sick," Steven repeated. His face was lost in his mind of memories. "I was sick. They came for me."

Puzzled, Freddy said, "Came for you? Who came for you, Steven?"

His voice soft, "I messed up. Somewhere, I messed up. They came."

"Who?" Freddy demanded. "Who came for you?"

Steven blared as he stood, his eyes bulging, "DEMONS! They came for me!"

Freddy, startled, slid back in the plastic lawn chair, legs screeching loudly as they scraped the linoleum. His hands were held out as silence fell on the room. The microwave light flickered in the background. Freddy let out a breath whispering, "Holy shit."

His voice came back, "Steven...Steven, listen, I'm sorry. It's...it's alright. Holy shit, you scared the crap out of me."

Steven slowly sat back down, and his eyes settled. "They came for me."

"Okay, yeah, they came. Got it." Freddy kept breathing heavy, his heart racing.

A minute passed in silence. Freddy got his breathing under control and stood up. Steven watched him. "It's alright. I'm gonna go get my phone. I'll be right back."

Freddy backed away to the door and Steven stared at him the entire time. When he closed the door, he let out the breath he was unconsciously holding. He darted to the embalming room and scooped up his phone on the counter. Freddy opened the screen, went to text messages, and texted George, GET OVER HERE NOW. BACKDOOR. RING BELL.

He closed the app and then opened a new one, hitting the record button. He placed the phone in his front pocket with the mic at the top.

Steven was still staring at the door when he came back in. "It's alright. Just me. Just Freddy." He made his way back to the chair and sat down.

Freddy said, "So, why did they, uh, the demons, come for you?" Freddy waited for the outburst from Steven, but it didn't come.

"To punish me."

"To punish you? Why?"

"I was wrong. I...I..."

"Wrong about what?"

Steven looked hard at Freddy. Freddy steeled himself for another outburst. Steven said, "You don't get it?" His eyes were angry. Then they softened, "They were right."

"Who was right?"

"He told us. We didn't listen."

Freddy didn't ask anything. He just waited for Steven to keep talking. None of what he said made any sense.

Steven's voice was matter of fact, "I am the way, the truth, the life. He was right."

Freddy felt the vibration of his phone. He received a text. Confirmation George received his. He got his courage back, "So, Steven, let's talk about the demons you mentioned. They came for you. Where did they take you?"

"Hell."

"Tell me what happened when you died."

Steven drifted back into his memory, "I lifted up into the air. I remember it being so beautiful. I could see...everyone. I saw myself on the grass. I couldn't hear anything at first. It was silent, peaceful." He swallowed hard. "Then I heard something. It was like a knife sliding against a metal pole. Screeching," his face soured at the memory. "I thought my eyes were seeing people drifting toward me. I was mesmerized by them. White angels, but no wings. Just white wispy looking cloth hiding faces beneath." He suddenly stopped and looked at Freddy.

Freddy was captivated and wanted to know what he saw. "What happened?"

Steven's eyes came alive, "Demons! Their faces..." His eyes narrowed, and he settled back in his chair. "They came for me. Slithery. Whispering voices of hate and violence. They wanted to shred my soul. They took me away...far away."

"To hell?" Freddy said.

"To hell!" His tone relaxed, "I can't go back...I can't."

"This is so crazy to me, Steven. So you are a hero, and yet they take you to hell? I don't get it."

Steven nonchalantly said, "They'll take you too."

Shivers ran down Freddy's spine.

"Unless..." Steven added.

"Unless, what?"

Steven began to cry. "They might come for me."

"Nobody is taking you anywhere. You're back from...hell." Freddy couldn't believe these words were coming from his own mouth.

Steven suddenly became animated, "How? How did I come back?"

Freddy, caught off guard by the question, said, "I don't know. It just happened."

"Tell me!" Steven edged closer to the table.

"I...I just said, get up and walk in Jesus' name. And you did. I don't know what happened. This," he pointed at Steven, "happened. You came back to life."

Steven settled back into his chair and whispered, "He answered you."

Freddy couldn't resist, "Who?"

Steven looked up at Freddy, his eyes glassy, head slightly tilted as if he was revealing a buried secret he promised never to say, "Jesus."

"So Christianity is true, then?"

Steven slouched back into his chair, "No, Jesus is true. Nothing else."

Freddy was trying to grapple with what he was seeing, what he was hearing. It was like he was caught inside *A Nightmare on Elm Street*. And Freddy Krueger was about to burst out of Steven in front of him with his bladed glove. He visualized Steven's chest, pushing outward, the face of Krueger stretching the skin out from his belly before puncturing through.

Freddy said, "Steven, this is, um...crazy. I'm not arguing with what just happened to you...I'm just...I'm just trying to comprehend it all."

Steven wasn't listening to Freddy. A sudden realization hit Steven's face and whispered, "I have a second chance."

"What do you mean?"

"I need forgiveness." Steven's voice rose, and he stood, "I need them to forgive me. I...I...I need to repent of...of...all of it. Yes...yes, that's it. I..." Steven's face slowly looked down at the leather belt he was clutching onto.

"What are you talking about? Forgive who?"

"No!" Steven turned to him. "I need them to forgive *me*!"

"Who?"

Steven threw the belt onto the table. The bronze metal of the buckle clattered with a hollow sound, the leather, a thud. It was twisted around like a snake. One side was plain brown with scuff marks here and there. The other had hash marks etched into it as if someone were marking how many days had passed. Steven pointed, "Them."

CHAPTER 33
FACING INNER DEMONS

FREDDY HELD THE old belt in his hand, inspecting the marks. "I don't understand, Steven. Who is this 'them' that you're referring to?"

Just before Steven answered, three successive thuds came from the back door, startled them both.

Freddy appeased Steven, "It's alright. I know who it is." He got up and went to the door. He opened it, and standing there was George Casey smiling brightly, holding his arms out wide. One hand held a bottle of scotch. The other held a shield. George was dressed in full costume as Captain America. "This party is going to be fucking epic," he said.

"Get in here," Freddy said in a harsh whisper.

George walked in and looked around the kitchen. This was his first time inside Freddy's workplace. Under his breath George said, "What a shithole."

Freddy spun him around to face him. "Why are you dressed up like that?"

"What do ya mean? We're having a secret party, right?"

"No shithead, we're not. How did you get "party" from my text?"

George went to answer, but Freddy cut him off, "Never mind, just follow me and don't say a word."

Freddy turned, walking toward the door to the hallway. Captain America followed. As Steven turned and saw them, his mouth fell open in shock. George stood tall, smiled, and gave him the Captain America salute as they passed by. Freddy held the door open until George was out, then closed it.

"George, listen to me. I don't...I don't even know where to fucking start."

George set his shield against the wall. He put his free hand on Freddy's shoulder, "Woah, woah, settle down, little-buddy. What the fuck's happening, dude? Just take a deep breath."

Freddy's voice lowered, "The guy in there," he pointed toward the kitchen. "I did it."

George's face scrunched in confusion, "You did what? And who the fuck is creepy fat guy in the kitchen?"

"This is crazy," Freddy said, his breathing labored.

"Just settle the fuck down, dude. Okay, here," George uncapped the scotch and said, "drink this."

Freddy took a swig and felt the heat of the liquor cascading down his throat. George said, "Good, now take another one, then tell me what the fuck's happening."

Freddy did as instructed. George took the bottle back and capped it. Freddy said, "That guy is Steven Murdock. He died two days ago from a heart attack." He let the statement rest.

George listened. His face was concerned. Fear began to edge inside him considering where he now stood, inside a morgue. Bodies were probably lined up behind him down the hall. This was a place he always wanted to visit. But at the same time, a place that scared the shit out of him.

George began to giggle, then said, "Okay, yeah, good one. Woah!" He placed his hand onto his chest. "You had me going there for a second. Woah, my heart is off to the fucking races." George saw Freddy's face didn't change. He knew his friend and he knew when he was serious and when he was joking. "You're fucking serious?"

"George, that guy was dead an hour ago."

George's eyes flared wide. He said loudly, "FUCK ME!" Freddy tried to cup his mouth, but it was too late. George went immediately to a whisper, "Sorry, sorry." He uncapped the scotch and took a drink. Freddy grabbed it and did the same. George gulped, "Is it a fucking zombie or something. Okay, I know what we need to do. We need to stab it in the head."

"No, you fucking idiot, it's not a zombie. His name is Steven Murdock. He saved a little girl a couple days ago and had a heart attack at the same time."

"How did this happen? It's obvious he didn't die."

"I checked his vitals. George," he slowed his words, "he was dead."

"So, what happened?"

"I don't know. It's like a blur. I saw a fucking video of a cockroach coming back to life, and then I put my hand down on...him," he pointed to the kitchen door, "and said, get up and walk." He waved his hands around, "And that's exactly what he fucking did. He got up and walked."

"Get up and walk, huh?" George's eyes narrowed under his mask, "Have you talked to him? Is he able to?"

"Yeah, he's fucking talking about heaven and hell kind of shit in there. My mind is all fucked up, now."

"Okay, so what do you want me to do? You want me to hold him down while you..."

Freddy was disgusted, "No, dude. I don't want you to hold him down."

"Sorry, I'm just trying to figure out what you want me to do."

"Just talk to him or something. I don't know. It's not like it's in any manual what to do when a fucking body comes back to life."

"Talk to him? What the fuck do you want me to talk to him about? How was it up there?"

Freddy pointed down.

George said, "He was in fucking hell?" He turned on his heels, "Now *I'm* in fucking hell."

"Just be you."

He turned back to look at Freddy, "Just be me, huh?"

"Yeah, ya know, George fucking Casey aka Captain fucking America."

"Funny."

They looked at each other for a long moment. Freddy said, "Well?"

"I'm fucking thinkin'." He took another swig of the scotch. "Okay, this is what we're gonna do." Freddy leaned in to hear the plan. George announced, "We're gonna fucking wing-it."

Freddy stepped back, "That's your fucking plan? Wing it?"

George smiled, "Trust me."

Freddy took a deep breath and exhaled, "Fine. Whatever." He followed George back into the kitchen.

Steven wasn't sitting down. He was standing in front of the microwave, staring at the malfunctioning light inside as it flashed on and off sporadically. George looked back at Freddy who shrugged.

"Hey, Steven," George started. He had a big grin on his face. "Steven, that's your·name, right? My name is George."

Steven said, "This reminds me of home."

"Okay, creepy," George said softly. "So, let's talk about home then. Do you want to sit down?"

Steven never looked away from the microwave. "Mom died twenty-one years ago."

George made his way to the kitchen table. "I'm sorry to hear that." George sat down.

"My dad died twenty years ago."

George turned his attention back to Steven, "Wow, you lost both your parents. I'm truly sorry, dude.

"I'm not."

George looked at Freddy with concern and mouthed, "I'm out

of here." Freddy grabbed George's shoulders, held him down and whispered, "Keep him going. You've got this." George flipped him off on the low. "Hey, Steven, wanna come over and sit down? Seems like you've had a rough day. I've got some scotch here."

Steven turned. Freddy retrieved plastic cups from the cabinet. Steven walked to the table, sliding his feet on the floor while George poured each of them a drink. Steven sat down and grabbed one. He sniffed it, then downed it.

George raised an eyebrow, "Well done." Then poured him another.

He downed that one as well.

George peeled off his Captain America mask, which looked like it came directly from the movie set. He placed it on the table. His orange-blond hair fell perfectly into place. George was about to ask him to retell his story when Steven said, "I have a second chance."

George diverted to that, "Alright, yeah, let's go with that. Second chance. Steven, um, second chance at what, my friend?"

"To be forgiven. To get right."

George looked up at Freddy who stood behind Steven. He refocused on Steven, "Yeah, forgiveness, that's the fucking best."

"You swear a lot," Steven chided.

"Um, oh, sorry, does that bother you? Of course, it does. Otherwise, you wouldn't have fu...I mean, said that."

"My mom swore. She swore at my dad."

George nodded his head and squinted.

Steven said, "He killed her."

George instantly stood up, "Alright, Freddy, might I have a word with you." He grabbed his arm and pulled him away from the table whispering, "This is fucking insanity. We need to call in a professional or something. Maybe fucking Dr. Beckman."

"No, no shrinks. It's fine. He's harmless."

"Harmless, the creepy fat guy who just came back from hell and dropped the fucking bomb his dad killed his mother? That's fucking harmless?"

"Alright, yeah...that kind of sounds off a bit," Freddy admitted. "But he was a hero, George. He saved the little girl. It doesn't mean he's like his dad."

George let go of his arm and straightened out his blue costume. He turned back to Steven, smiled, and then sat back down at the table. "Well, this getting to know you talk is really something, Steven. Um, why don't we talk about something else, what kind of sports you like to play or something." George winced and instantly regretted his question looking at how well Steven took care of himself.

Steven answered, "Tetherball. I liked that game."

George let out a sigh, "Oh yeah," then looked at Freddy, "tetherball. That's a good fu...that's a great sport. I loved that one too."

Steven said, "Checkers."

George smiled, "What about chess?"

Steven glared at him sharply, "My dad liked chess. Said it made you smart."

George's smile soured instantly.

Steven grumbled, "He said I was dumb."

"No, you're not dumb. Sometimes people say things they don't mean."

"He told me I was stupid every morning before school."

"Well, that's...not right." George backed off the subject.

Steven continued, "He told me I was the reason he killed mom."

George didn't respond. Freddy held his breath.

"He told me I would never be anything in life but a retard." Steven was getting worked up as he relived the painful memories. "He told me he hated me and wished I were dead."

Silence fell on the room.

George and Freddy looked at one another. Concern on their faces. They turned back to Steven.

"Twenty years ago," Steven's voice became solemn. "I killed him."

CHAPTER 34
THANK YOU FOR COMING

GEORGE SPRANG FROM his chair, "Okay, yeah, Steven, uh, thank you for coming. It's been a pleasure." He turned and said under his breath, "Not really." He planted his hand on Freddy's chest and pushed him to the door.

Before they went through it, Steven began to sputter and sniffle. The beginnings of a deep cry. His face fell into his awaiting hands. He sobbed.

Freddy said, "We need to help him, dude."

"No fucking way. He just admitted to killing his dad." He held up two fingers, "And his amazing father killed his mom! I'm not about to get next in line, if you know what I mean."

"This guy was dead, and now he's not."

"Dude, what if this is the way zombies start? Maybe he's patient zero and shit. He could bite one of us."

Annoyed, Freddy said, "Bite us?" He pushed past his friend, "He's not a zombie."

George reluctantly followed, "He could be."

Freddy went to Steven and trepidly placed a hand on his shoulder. "It's alright. Let it out, Steven. We're here for you."

Through muffled tears, "I killed them. I was wrong." He kept repeating it.

George mouthed to Freddy, "Fucking zombie."

Freddy shook his head, then went back to consoling Steven. "It's alright."

George smacked his forehead, spun around, and walked a few steps away.

A minute passed and Steven stopped crying. Snot and tears dripped from his hands. Freddy snapped his fingers to George, pointing to the roll of paper towels. George caught on and grabbed the roll, handing it to Freddy before backing away. Freddy tore several sheets off and gave them to Steven, who took them and wiped his face.

George's back was turned away as he whispered, "Fuck, fuck, fuck, fuck, fuck."

Steven said with venom, "Stop swearing!"

George brought up his hands in surrender, "Sorry, sorry. Yeah, check, no swearing."

Steven looked at the microwave. He stared at it. The light flickered. He said, "It reminds me of my TV at home."

Freddy looked at George, who shrugged.

Steven continued while he fell into another trance-like state, "It told me things."

George mocked, "Yep, TV's have a way of telling us things."

Freddy put his finger to his mouth, aggravated with George.

Steven said, "The voices calmed me."

George made a 'this guy is psycho' gesture with his hand. Freddy shook his head to stop.

Steven said, "They gave me direction." He suddenly turned and looked up at Freddy, "I have to feed my rats."

Freddy quickly said, "Your rats are fine. We can't go just yet."

"Why?"

"Because…" he looked at George for help. "Cause…George is a doctor, and he needs to clear you."

George rolled his eyes in disbelief at what his best friend had just told this murderer. He snapped back into a smile when Steven looked at him. "Yes," he cleared his throat and tried to sound like a doctor, "need to clear you."

Steven waited.

George looked at Freddy. Freddy said, "Looks like a mild disorientation syndrome, MDS, right doctor?"

"Yeah, that's right, MDS. It's rare but considering you came back from hell and all. It…it can happen."

Steven agreed, "I'm a little disoriented."

"Okay," George sat down again, "Let's see his chart, Freddy."

"Right, chart. Let me get it."

"It's not here?"

"No, it's in the embalming room. I'll be right back."

George stood, panic on his face, "No, negative. MDS requires two people in the room at all times. We will go together."

Freddy said slowly, "O-k-a-y."

George kept facing Steven as they walked to the hallway door. Steven stared at him.

They were in the hallway.

George's two hands shot up, "Just when I'm trying to get the fuck out, you drag me back into this. What kind of friend are you?"

Freddy pulled his phone out of his front shirt pocket. "It's recording. We get him admitting to everything, and then we can turn him in."

George froze, "Great plan, and then they fucking arrest me for pretending to be a fucking doctor."

"It's the best I got." Freddy walked away.

George followed him into the embalming room.

"Do you have any weapons?" George asked.

Freddy ignored him and grabbed Steven's chart off the counter.

Meanwhile, George found a scalpel close by on the floor and picked it up. "Better than nothing." He tucked it under his blue leather armor.

"Okay," George said, "What's the new plan?"

"I don't know."

"You don't know."

"Alright, alright. Um, get him talking about his belt. Yeah, his belt."

"Belt?"

"Yeah, he was clutching his belt ever since he came back. He seems pretty attached to it. There are some markings on it."

"Markings?"

"Yeah, just...do—"

"Do...what?"

"Whatever you think of." Freddy walked out.

"Whatever I think of," George repeated and then followed.

They walked into the kitchen as Steven was about to exit the back door. Freddy yelled, "Steven, wait, what are you doing?"

He turned, "I wanted to see where I'm at and...and get some air."

"No, no, no, um, fresh air is bad. Right doctor?"

Steven said, "It is?"

"Yeah," George jumped in. "Yeah, the fresh air can worsen your disorientation. You need oxygen, and this place is pumping in pure, clean oxygen. Don't, don't go out there."

Steven retracted his hand from the door's crash-bar.

"Come on and sit down," Freddy instructed him back to the chair. He complied.

George sat opposite and took the chart Freddy handed him. "Okay," he kept repeating as he scanned over the information. Nothing jumped out at him. "So, you love your belt, it says here," he lied. "Tell me about your belt."

Steven's blank stare caused George to shift uncomfortably in his chair. "Steven, you there? You alright?"

Steven continued to stare and then asked, "Are you really a doctor?"

George looked at Freddy in shock.

"You're not dressed like one."

George laughed, "Oh, yeah, this is a costume. It's Halloween. I got called over from a party and didn't have time to change."

"My dad said Halloween was stupid like me."

George looked concerned again.

Steven kept talking, "Children would come to our house, but we were never home."

"Where were you?" George asked.

"At our other home. The home nobody knew about. It's where mom and dad are." Steven rubbed his eyes and face. He looked at Freddy, "My rats are there."

"It's alright. They're fine."

Steven went into deep thought again. He looked at Freddy, who stood off to the side and leaned against the kitchen counter. "Do you think they will forgive me?"

"I'm not sure who you're talking about. Forgive you for what?"

"I killed them."

Freddy looked at George, then responded, "You said your dad killed your mom, and you then killed your dad. You keep saying "them." I think your mom and dad were messed up people, Steven. I think they would want to forgive you if they could."

Steven shook his head, "No, not them. The others."

Freddy moved closer, "What others?"

George was frozen in place.

Steven said, "The other moms and dads."

CHAPTER 35
SEETHING

GEORGE AND FREDDY looked hard at one another, caught in utter surprise, unable to move. Their stomachs lurched, pulses raced. This had escalated to a whole new level. George wasn't feeling like a fake doctor anymore but, unfortunately now, like a fake homicide detective.

Freddy asked, "Why do you need forgiveness from the other moms and dads?"

George didn't want to ask the question Freddy just asked, but it was the very question at the forefront of his mind. It was like a train wreck you couldn't stop watching. Even worse was the upcoming answer from Steven. George now considered him to be a psychopath. The answer couldn't possibly be good. He had already admitted to killing his own father and he talked about pet rats. He talked about a private home no one knew about. The answer forthcoming was guaranteed to add to this deranged list.

Steven answered like he was just asked by a teacher what two plus two was, "For taking their children to a new home."

George swallowed hard and began to sweat under the leather and polyester costume. Freddy let out the breath he was holding. He held up a hand to calm George.

Freddy asked, "What new home, Steven? Where is this home?"

Again, Steven answered like it was no big deal, "To heaven."

"Oh shit!" George yelled and stood up while grabbing his hair.

"How many did you send to heaven?" Freddy said.

Steven pointed to the belt on the table.

"Holy shit!" George yelled again. His hands planted to each side of his head.

"Stop swearing!" Steven responded.

George didn't care. He reached for his cell phone and looked at Freddy, "It's over, dude. I have to."

Freddy nodded his agreement.

"Who are you calling?" Steven asked.

He narrowed his eyes, "Who do you think? The fucking police, dude."

Steven suddenly stood, shoving the plastic table into George, whose phone slipped out of his hand by the surprise attack. It slid on the floor. Steven cried out, "No police! Ever!"

George slammed into the back wall, pinned by the table Steven kept pushing against him. George slid out the scalpel hidden in his costume and slashed at Steven. He missed. Steven, with great hidden agility, grabbed George's arm holding the weapon with one hand. He then backhanded him with his other. George went flying to his right, hitting his head on the edge of another counter. He slumped to the ground unconscious, blood coming out of a gash on his head.

Steven turned toward Freddy, ready for a fight.

Freddy held out his hands in surrender, "I'm not gonna hurt you."

Steven slapped his head and face over and over, crazed. "You can't hurt me. Nothing can hurt me. I'm invincible."

Freddy looked around for a weapon. Nothing. He knew there were dull knives in a drawer nearby, but Steven would easily get to him before that. Everything happened so fast. He was trying to get his bearings. His friend was on the floor across from him, bleeding. Steven was in between.

Steven said, "Will they forgive me or not?"

Freddy, panic-stricken, kept the conversation going, "I don't know." He remembered his phone was recording everything, "What did you do?"

"I have a second chance. I came back from hell! Will they forgive me?"

Freddy yelled, "What did you do?"

The words that fell from Steven's mouth slowed down. They couldn't register in Freddy's mind as the whirlwind of events unraveled. Steven's voice was soft and pleasant, "I set them free to become angels."

The word he used could have been a trigger, but it was the way he said it. Free to become angels. Freddy knew they caught the Angel Killer weeks ago. The woman in red at George's party was from the media and said they might have caught the wrong guy. Who was Steven Murdock? What atrocities had he committed? Why did God allow him to come back? He belonged in hell.

"Angels?" Freddy whispered.

"They said I was a killer, but I wasn't," Steven's voice began to crack with emotion. "They said it, over and over and over again on TV, but it wasn't true. They didn't know."

"Are you...?" Freddy struggled.

"They judged me," Steven continued. "They said horrible things about me. My father said I was an idiot and stupid."

"Are you...?

"I birthed angels, but they called me,"

"Are you...?

"The Angel Killer."

Freddy stopped breathing. His vision blurred. It felt like someone punched him in the stomach and testicles at the same time. It wasn't possible. It couldn't be happening. He must be imagining it all. This wasn't real. The flickering light of the microwave intensified as the room began to spin. Steven's pudgy face stretched closer to him like he was inside a psych ward on massive drugs.

"You...you...you," Freddy stuttered.

"I'm not an Angel Killer."

"You...you...killed...her."

"Will the moms and dads forgive me? I just want to know."

"You...killed...my."

"I just want to know," he cried.

"Daughter."

Steven's face tilted to the side like a dog hearing an unfamiliar sound. His tears immediately dried up. He narrowed his eyes at him, "What's your name?"

"Foley...Freddy Foley," he squeezed out of his pursed lips.

Steven thought about the name. He bent down to pick up his belt, lying at his feet. He turned it over to reveal the individual marks. He pointed to mark number fourteen. Everyone thought she was number twelve, but they hadn't found the others yet. Steven was lost in the memories of his victims. Reliving his actions over and over until reaching the name buried within him. He memorized them all. Steven knew them intimately. His TV told him who they were. He collected the newspapers and magazines and piled them high within the hidden home where his mom and dad's skeletal remains rested.

The name fell from Steven's lips, "Evelyn."

Freddy stumbled, and his hand caught him on the counter. His eyes glassed over. He croaked out the words, "Nooo...nooo." Spit dribbled down his chin. "Nooo." This couldn't be happening. Steven wasn't in hell. He was. There wasn't life after death. There was just more pain. Everyone was destined for pain. But pain wasn't the right word. Torture. Everyone was destined to be tortured.

Steven fell to his knees. He lifted his hands. His belt hanging from one of them. He cried out to Freddy, "Forgive me? Please forgive me. I have a second chance."

Freddy clutched the counter. He heard the psychopath who killed his daughter crying out for forgiveness. It was all in slow motion. His voice slowed and gurgled like the movies. Freddy's hand touched something on the counter. He looked. The light flickered in his face as he looked at his reflection in the microwave door. Freddy grabbed the microwave with a sudden surge of anger. With both hands, he lifted it into the air and then threw it at Steven. The microwave slammed into his face, knocking him out. Blood came out of a cut on his forehead and his broken nose.

The microwave light, after years of tormenting him, was finally off.

Freddy stumbled over to George. He barely got out the words, "I'm here. It's alright." Freddy got up and went into the hallway. He needed to get the first aid kit. He had one in his office.

Stumbling, he went to his desk and pulled open the lower drawer. The white first-aid box was there. Freddy grabbed it and stumbled back to the kitchen, exhausted and in a daze. He was moving on pure fumes of adrenaline. He opened the kitchen door. George was there. Steven was gone.

He saw blood on the floor. Another drop at his feet. His eyes followed the trail leading down the hallway to Pinewood offices. The Angel Killer was still alive and somewhere inside. Freddy went to his friend, pulling out the gauze. He cleaned the cut with the antiseptic wipe the best he could and then quickly wrapped his head with the gauze. Blood was saturating through the meshed material, but it would have to do for now. George was out cold, but he was alive. This wasn't George's fight. It was his. "You rest up, Captain America. I've got this one."

Freddy didn't realize his fist was clenched. He didn't realize his face was turning bright red. He was beyond anger. He was seething. God had answered his prayer. The Angel Killer would be on his table this very night, and he would embalm him alive.

Freddy stood and walked in a trance toward his office. Head down. Eyes glaring ahead.

He quoted his favorite movie in a whisper, "1-2-Freddy's coming for you…"

CHAPTER 36
FREDDY KRUEGER VS THE
ANGEL KILLER

REDDY WALKED OPPOSITE from where Steven had run off to. Freddy's face was set like flint—purposed, unwavering in his intent—steeled in anger. He walked directly to his office, stopping in the doorway. His eyes connected with the item on his desk encased in glass.

Suddenly, the entire building went black. Steven had obviously cut the power. The back-up generators turned on the emergency lights. The generator's main purpose was to keep the refrigeration units going to maintain the bodies, but the red glow of the emergency lights cast eerie shadows within the hallways. The red light in his office illuminated the item like a prize. Freddy was no longer Frederick Foley. His mind shattered. He took off the glass covering and set it down on his desk. His eyes never left the object under the glass dome. Slowly, his hands wrapped around it and lifted it from its pedestal. The infamous bladed glove replica from *A Nightmare on Elm Street* would be the perfect weapon to cause extreme pain and exact his vengeance.

Seething rage washed away any capacity for thinking clearly. Freddy's persona became that of his beloved childhood villain, Freddy Krueger. He placed his right hand inside the glove. The velcro strap stretched around his wrist to lock it in place. He played with the bladed fingers, getting used to them, extending them out in front of his face and a slight smile began to form on his lips. The red light from the darkened room cast shadows across him, accentuating his evil intent.

Freddy pulled out his custom-made bladed thimble and put it into his pocket.

"Now your time is up, motherfucker."

He stepped back into the hallway and looked to his right, which headed down to offices and circled left to the front lobby. The conference and casket rooms were situated in the middle of Pinewood. On the complete opposite end from where he stood was the chapel room. There were plenty of places to hide and multiple exits. But when Steven cut the power, he also set the exit doors to lock. No one was leaving unless they had Freddy's clearance code. Freddy knew this building like the back of his hand and Steven had never been here before. Freddy went to his right to circle around instead of following where Steven had originally gone. He was deathly silent as he stalked his prey.

He took in the glass windows with shadowy cubicles behind them. Softly glowing red emergency lights in the corners and the outside street lamplight cascaded in as he passed by the Mortuary and Cemetery sales offices. He peered left at the corner of the hallway. Everything was quiet. Bathrooms on his left. Admin and Manager offices to the right. Just beyond was the reception and lobby. He made his way down the corridor until he was finally standing in the middle of the square lobby room. The front glass doors and windows showed the parking lot outside. The chapel was to his left as he looked out the front. Behind him were the viewing and casket rooms.

He took a step toward the chapel when he heard a sudden, hollow thump to his left. He looked down the creepy hallway of the viewing and casket rooms. Another thump. It was further down. He walked toward the noise. Another thump. He knew Steven was in the casket room. With confidence, he slid the bladed glove along the right wall, leaving scratch marks behind. His blades slid across the metal doors too, making a loud screeching noise.

He stood in front of the door labeled Casket Room and Urn Samples, then opened it. Freddy said, "You took everything from me." He stepped in. It was dark except for a single emergency red light in the far corner. Caskets lined the walls and flanked the middle. To his left and right were urn samples in glass cases. Several caskets were toppled over, which had created the thuds he heard before. He squinted as he looked into the shadows beyond. A figure emerged. Still. Staring at him.

Steven's voice echoed from back in the room, "Forgive me. I beg of you."

"What kind of sick fuck kills children?"

"I went to hell because of it, Mr. Foley." Steven began to cry.

"You're going to go back, motherfucker, because of it." He slid his blades across a casket as he made his way toward Steven, who stood in the back shadows, five rows back. The claws dug into the finished wood, creating eerie sounds with every scrape.

"What is that noise?" Steven asked.

Freddy said, his lips pursed in pure unadulterated hatred, "Forgiveness."

"Yes, thank you. I'll tell you everything. Just forgive me."

"It's coming."

"She died quickly."

Freddy stopped cold in his tracks. Another attack on his psyche. "Don't talk about her," he managed to squeak out.

"She's an angel, Freddy. She's free now."

"Don't...talk...about...her, EVER!" The rage he fought so many years to temper now boiled to the surface. He was three rows away from him. Caskets toppled over, forcing him to go in a snakelike fashion toward Steven's motionless body standing in the back shadows.

"Just forgive me, Freddy. I don't want to go back."

"Why did you kill my little girl?" he whispered.

"She was special. She was chosen."

Freddy's voice was soft as he continued the conversation. He needed to know why. "Yeah, special and chosen. By who? Who told you these things? Your dead father?"

"God told me. He speaks to me."

"And your god thanked you by sending you to hell?"

"I must have done something wrong."

"Why don't you ask him? He talks to you, right?"

"I've tried," he cried. "I can't hear...him."

"Eve spoke to me. Did you know that?"

Steven stopped crying. "She's an angel now," he said.

Freddy was two rows away as he slowly made his way toward Steven. "She was always an angel. She didn't need any fucking help from you."

"What did she say?"

Freddy didn't answer. He chuckled. A hideous chilling scoff. "Ever think that you weren't hearing God, but instead your own fucking psychotic thoughts? Have you?"

Silence.

Freddy said, "What's the matter? Did...did you not like that question? I mean, your dad called you a fucking loser. Maybe something snapped inside that tiny fucking brain of yours, and you suddenly clearly heard the voice of fucking God. I mean, really? You? Hearing God? God created the entire fucking universe, and He decided to talk to you. And told you to fucking kill little kids? He told you to take them away from their parents? God wanted you, a pimple on an asshole, to take an innocent life and turn them into an angel?"

He was one row away. He could see the fat silhouette of the piece of shit that killed his daughter. Freddy had talked himself into a calm. He was holding the storm back, waiting to unleash his full fury when he could reach him. The storm stalked Steven, who waited on the other side for him.

"You know what I think?" Freddy continued, "I think you killed your dad cause he hurt you so much. He probably killed your mom, as you said, but deep down, that wasn't the reason why you turned the way you did. I mean, really, we would have serial killers in every household if it were because our daddy's told us we were a loser. My dad beat the shit out of me for looking at him wrong. I didn't kill him. Might have thought of doing it once. He called me a loser a few times over the years. I didn't have to kill him, Steven. He fucking killed himself. Drank himself to death. My mom?" he laughed, "Well, yeah, she was fucking mother of the year. Left me and dad when I was ten." Freddy paused. No response from Steven. "So, why am I fucking telling you all of this, Steven? Based on your reality, God should have started talking to me and telling me to slice up little kids or something."

Freddy turned the last row. Six feet away was Steven. He was positioned in the shadows, and Freddy couldn't make out any details. It didn't matter. All he saw was a fat slug of a man who deserved to go back to hell.

Freddy said, "Yeah, you're a piece of shit. In fact, you're worth less than a piece of shit."

Steven finally said something, "What did Eve say to you?"

"Psychopathic motherfuckers like you don't get to hear what daughters say to their dad's. All you fucking hear is your insanity inside your mind. You didn't care then, and you sure as hell don't care now."

"I need to know. What did she say?"

Freddy scoffed, "You want to know, huh? I'll tell you what she said." Freddy charged forward, raised his weaponized hand, and said, "She told me to send you back to hell, motherfucker!" His blades slashed downward, cutting into Steven. Steven's body was hard and rigid and fell backward, revealing the ruse. It was a mannequin covered with a blanket.

Freddy felt the sharp pain at the back of his head and then shards of pottery falling around him as Steven bashed him with an urn. Freddy fell to the ground, reaching for his head while turning toward Steven, who stood over him, heaving large breaths. Steven held a jagged fragment of the urn in his hand. Freddy lurched forward and slashed Steven's leg open with four clean cuts. Blood splashed to the ground as it drained from each wound. Steven cried out in pain and fell down, holding his leg.

Both of them got back to their feet, wobbling. Freddy slashed at him again, hitting his shoulder. Steven pushed through the pain and tried to hit Freddy with the urn piece, but Freddy dodged the pathetic attack and countered with a puncture to his gut. Steven stumbled backward. The blade stuck into Steven, ripping from the glove. Steven turned and ran away, stumbling into coffins along the way until finally reaching the exit from the room.

Freddy leaned against a casket and breathed heavily. His face scrunched in pain as his free hand grabbed his head where Steven had struck him.

The live embalming process had begun. Eight slices to slowly drain the blood and one puncture into the stomach. *"Not the best job I've ever done,"* he thought to himself. But Freddy had never felt more alive embalming this one.

He stumbled the way Steven had fled and said, "Let's finish this."

CHAPTER 37
LIFE OR DEATH

FREDDY FOLLOWED THE trail of blood. In some spots, it was smeared from Steven dragging his bare feet. He looked at his clawed hand. Only three blades remained of the four. The index finger blade was buried into Steven's gut. His replica was holding up fairly well, considering it wasn't truly designed to slice people up as the movie portrayed. Judging by the amount of blood, however, Freddy didn't think Steven could go much further.

"Fuck it," he removed the glove and tossed it to the side. He reached in his pocket for his customized bladed thimble—the sharpest blade in his arsenal. He attached it to his finger, secured it with the wrap between his thumb and palm, and walked on.

"I'm coming for ya, Steven. You're bleeding out, you sick fuck."

Freddy pushed open the door that connected two hallways. He was back to the original hallway where this nightmare began. To his right was the chapel. To his left was the garage, kitchen, and at the far end, the embalming room. The blood trail went off to his left. Walking carefully to avoid the slippery pools of blood, he came to the embalming room. The door was closed. To the left, the hallway continued. The next door down was his office.

Freddy took notice of the blood that was sloshed all around—some leading down the hallway toward his office. The embalming room door was closed, but the blood trail also led inside. The entire area was filled with foot and hand marks spread about to confuse him.

"Very clever," he said under his breath. He said louder, "It's only a matter of time, asshole. I'll either find you alive or dead. It's up to you."

Freddy decided to check the embalming room first. He opened the door and looked into the dimly lit area. He waited for sounds of breathing. The loss of that much blood would intensify Steven's breathing, forcing him to breath harder to compensate. He saw the table toppled over where Steven once lay dead and then miraculously came back to life. Embalming tools littered the ground. It was darker in this room because there was only one emergency light, which was partially blocked due to an extra set of storage cabinets installed in that corner. He could barely make out the blood trail heading further into the darkness. Freddy squinted his eyes, trying to discern what lay in wait for him. He slowly took one step further in.

Something hit him from behind and Steven tackled Freddy to the ground. He grabbed Freddy's arm and twisted it behind him while his fat and bleeding body lay on top, keeping him pinned down. Freddy attempted to squirm out, but it was futile. Steven leaned in and put more pressure on Freddy's face, now pressed hard against the tile floor.

Steven whispered, "My daddy taught me how to fight. Did your daddy do that?"

Freddy coughed out with labored breaths, "Get off me, you sick fuck!"

"I didn't want to fight," Steven rambled, "and he called me an idiot. He called me stupid. He said they would kill me if I didn't fight. He was right."

Freddy struggled to breathe as Steven's weight pressed the life out of him. "You're breaking my arm," he struggled to say.

"My daddy said you fight to win. When you have a gun, you shoot to kill. When you have a knife, you gut to kill. Your daddy didn't teach you that. You didn't kill me." Steven's voice was calm, with a hint of superiority.

"All I wanted," Steven continued, "was forgiveness. He gave me a second chance. But if you won't forgive, then there is no need to keep you around."

"Fuck you!"

"Momma always hated dad for swearing. She would beat my hide good if I ever swore. She said it was the devil's tongue."

"You're the...devil!" he gritted out.

"She told him to take that devil tongue and leave. You know what he did?" Steven waited for Freddy to respond, but he didn't. "Well, of course, you don't know. I never said, and you were never there." Steven lightened up just a tad. Just enough to allow Freddy more oxygen. He coughed and sputtered, sucking in what little air he could.

Steven leaned back in and whispered, "My daddy got a hammer and bashed her head in. He made me watch. He said this would happen to me if I didn't obey him."

Steven thought for a moment before saying, "You know what? My daddy was god to me. I did everything he told me. But then I started hearing a new voice. The voice of the true god. He told me things that would happen, and sure enough, they did. I saw things in my mind and watched them happen right on my very own TV. He told me I would be saving people and helping expand his kingdom."

"Get off of me, you sick fuck!"

Steven leaned in, "Your language, Mr. Foley." Freddy choked in pain.

Steven continued, "God told me I would help him build his angel army to battle the dark forces of this world. So I told my daddy, and he beat me good. I had the bruises to prove it, yes I did." Steven chuckled at the thought. "Yeah, he needed convincing just like I did. That was my fault, and I deserved my thrashing that day. So the next time I heard the voice of god, I told daddy what I had heard and said watch the TV to see for himself. Wanna know what happened, Mr. Foley?"

Freddy gasped and struggled.

"Well, you guessed it, it happened exactly as my god said it would. My daddy became a believer that day."

"You're gonna die…" Freddy coughed, "no matter what."

As if Steven wasn't listening to him, he continued on, "Oh, the first couple of angels we birthed together. You see, no one knows about them. No, they only think I got fourteen, but you saw my belt, Mr. Foley. Sixteen. Those two were never found, just the way god instructed my daddy and me."

Freddy squawked out, "You fuckin psycho." Spittle ran down his mouth into the pool of blood that pressed, wet and sticky, against the side of his face.

Steven let out a big breath, "I'm tired, Mr. Foley. Tired of the running. My dog days are over. But you did me one favor before I go."

Freddy couldn't respond. He was trying to manage every breath he could as his life was slowly leaving.

Steven said, "You see, when you spilled my blood, that's what I needed in order to hear clearly. There has to be a sacrifice. Blood for sight. Blood for life. Blood for death." He coughed.

More pain wracked Freddy's body from the jostle.

"My blood, Mr. Foley, opened up the airwaves. I heard him," Steven said. "You know what he told me?" Steven leaned in and whispered, "He wants you, Mr. Foley."

Steven let up a little and allowed Freddy to take a breath. Freddy inhaled deeply, coughing and sputtering. Then Steven leaned in and got up close to his ear. He whispered, "I find it ironic, don't you, that god entwined our destiny to be here in this place at this exact moment. I saw you in the park that night. You saw me as well. Early morning. Foggy." He softly laughed. "How pathetic. You found me. The same place I had released your daughter into glory two years prior. You were blinded by anger." He chuckled, "Perhaps I'm blinded by duty." Steven's voice was getting softer. His weight on top of Freddy getting heavier.

Freddy knew Steven was dying. The loss of blood. Freddy knew he was dying too. He couldn't move; he couldn't breathe. His arm was pinned behind him. His face planted into the tile floor. His other hand was free, but he had felt around and found nothing to grab hold of.

His strength dwindled, as did any chance of his survival. But his hope ignited knowing the Angel Killer would die before he did.

Steven said, "I like you, Mr. Foley. I wish we could have been friends. It's unfortunate you can't see the truth. You just can't see...the truth."

More weight fell upon Freddy. He cringed in pain. What little air he could muster was forced out of him. He felt his arm on the verge of breaking.

"Before I go to be with my maker," Steven added, "I will send you on your way, Mr. Foley. Give my regards to the demons in hell that await you." Steven leaned in hard on Freddy. Freddy's free hand stretched out as if to reach for life itself, fingers extended, only to come up empty-handed. His eyes bulged as his life flashed before him. He saw Jenny. He heard her voice, *"I told you to let it go."* Then George, *"You fucked up, buddy."* And finally, his daughter, *"Daddy, you didn't save me."*

Before he blacked out, a new voice emerged. "You first, asshole!" He knew that voice. Steven let out a gurgled scream then rolled off of Freddy and lay motionless at his side—staring directly at Freddy—shock captured in his lifeless eyes like an eerie black and white snapshot. Blood oozed out of his eardrum from the scalpel embedded into and now protruding from his left ear.

Someone grabbed Freddy and rolled him over. His vision was blurry.

"You alright?" he asked. The voice sounded distant.

Freddy groggily got out, "George?"

George was a sight. Blood-spattered gauze wrapped haphazardly around his head. A strand of it dangling all the way down to his blue spandex covered waist.

"Yeah, I'm here, buddy. I've got you." George helped Freddy to sit up. He sat next to him and allowed Freddy to lean into his chest. George rocked him as he held Freddy in his arms. "I've got you, buddy," he whispered. "Just breathe. It's alright. It's over."

Freddy thought, *"Was it over?"* He had lost everything. His daughter, his wife, his mind. Was it over for him? The reality started trickling in. The Angel Killer was dead. He was free from seeing any more killings on the news from him ever again. How many lives had they saved? There was no forgiveness to be found inside of Freddy. Only vengeance. And it was paid in full.

His friend rocked him back and forth. "It's alright. Just rest," George whispered.

Freddy said in a raspy voice, "I'm getting fucking seasick. Stop rocking."

George chuckled, "You got it, my friend. Good to hear your voice."

"Good to hear yours."

George held him for a minute more in silence.

Freddy finally said, "He's dead, right?"

George peered over at the lifeless body of the infamous Angel Killer. "Yeah, he's gone."

"Why don't I feel any different?"

"I don't know. Maybe tomorrow."

"Why tomorrow?"

George shrugged, "I don't know. I might throw a party or something."

"A party?"

"Yeah, why not?"

"But why?"

"Cause it's fucking Tuesday. Cause I lived to see another day. Cause—"

"Okay, okay, I got your point."

They were quiet for another moment. Freddy said, "It might be my last party. It better be a good one."

"Why?"

"They're gonna fuckin arrest me, dude."

"Why, it was self-defense, Freddy. He's the fucking Angel Killer."

"Nobody knows that. Everyone thinks this guy is a hero. We got cameras all over this place. I went after him."

George sighed, "Fuck."

They both were exhausted. Their voices were sluggish.

George said, "Well, at least you'll get fed three meals a day. I'll fucking visit you on the weekends. I'll have shared custody with you and the prison."

"Shared custody?"

"I've got good fucking lawyers. I'll get you weekends. They'll figure it out."

Freddy tried a half-hearted laugh, but it turned into a cough.

"Easy there, buddy. Save your energy," George consoled him.

"George," Freddy got serious.

"Yeah."

"Take care of Jenny for me. She deserved so much better."

"You're a fucking idiot."

"I know."

"No, you idiot. I'm saying she got what she deserved. The fucking best. She got my best friend."

"Just take care of her like you've taken care of me."

"Done."

"Thank you, Captain America."

They fell silent again.

Freddy asked, "How do you feel knowing you killed the Angel Killer?"

"I didn't kill him. You did."

Freddy leaned over to peer behind George. "I see a scalpel in his ear. It's not mine. I didn't put it there. Pretty sure your fingerprints are on that puppy." He fell back into George's arms.

"I don't know what you're talking about. I was just helping him with his hearing problem."

"Oh, hearing problem was it?"

"Actually, I was trying to hit his mouth to have him shut the fuck up. My vision was a little blurry at the time."

Freddy chuckled.

George rambled on, "He's probably fucking thanking me right now."

"How do you figure that?"

"He probably didn't want to hear all the demons down there talking smack. He'll just turn his head now to his bad ear."

Freddy tried to laugh, "Oh, fuck, that hurts." He placed his hand on his chest, grimacing in pain. He said after it settled, "That's a good one."

"Well, you know what they say about me, right?"

"Remind me."

"I'm a fucking giverrrrr!"

CHAPTER 38
NEVER SLEEP AGAIN

A s THEY SAT in the red glow of the emergency lights, Freddy
stirred.

George said, "Easy there, tiger."

"George, some serious shit is coming our way from all of this.
Serious for me...and for you."

"I know," he resigned.

"What if we could change that?"

George waited for an explanation.

"We could erase everything. Clean this place. Tonight."

George slowly nodded as the idea sunk in. "Fuck it. What do we
need to do?"

"First, let's get the power back on."

Freddy and George got up and hobbled down the hallway to the
electrical box at the far end. They popped open the lid and Freddy
lifted the main power switch. All the lights turned on.

"Now what?" George asked.

"Now we get to cleaning it all up. Blood...body...everything."

"Where do we start?"

"Body."

They hobbled back to the embalming room. Steven lay motionless with a pool of blood around him to their right. It all was so different now with the bright lights, less scary. Steven, the fat shell of the man, now looked sad. So much pain he had endured and caused Freddy and the other families over twenty years. Freddy snapped back out of his thoughts. He lifted up the stainless-steel table.

"Help me lift him."

George went to lift the corpse from the arms and shoulders while Freddy went to the legs. George looked away in discomfort from Steven's gruesome face and the scalpel still protruding from his ear.

"On three. One...two...three." They both heaved him up and onto the table.

"Deadweight is no joke," George commented through labored breaths.

Freddy nodded as he tried to catch his breath and then leaned down to start picking up the littered tools.

George said, "Are you going to embalm him?"

"No, we're going to incinerate him." Freddy pointed to the far door in the room. It was labeled CREMATORY.

George nodded, "Fuck yeah."

Freddy said, "Can you hand me those over there?" He pointed to forceps on the counter.

George grabbed them and handed them across the corpse to Freddy. Suddenly, Steven's hand grabbed George's arm. With his other hand, he pulled out the scalpel protruding from his ear and then stabbed George in the forearm.

It all happened in the blink of an eye. Steven screamed in pain from pulling the item from his eardrum. George countered Steven's scream with his own as he reflexively retreated with the scalpel now protruding from his arm.

Freddy tried to punch Steven in the face, but Steven grabbed his fist in his hand after letting go of George. Steven squeezed his hand with tremendous strength. It was crippling, forcing him to fall to his knees. Steven had intense rage on his bloodied face, gritting his teeth. The Angel Killer trembled as he pulled on some sort of demonic inner strength to dominate Freddy and force him to the ground. He sat up and pulled Freddy back to a standing position. Freddy struggled with the pain of his fist being crushed and heard a finger bone break.

"You...can't...win!" Steven said through gritted teeth.

"Fuck you!" Freddy said while reaching with his free hand to grasp the custom bladed thimble from his pocket. In one swift move, he sliced open the right side of Steven's neck. Steven released his grip, grabbing at his new wound. Blood sloshed through his fingers as he gurgled and fought to find air. His face became plastered with shock.

Freddy stood with renewed determination. He grabbed a long clear tube near him and lay it down on Steven's chest. Freddy, in clear vision, removed Steven's bloody hands away. He dug into his neck until he found what he was looking for, the carotid artery. He sliced it clean with his finger scalpel, placed the tube on one end of the revealed artery, and hit the ON button of the pump he knew was on a backup generator. The embalming fluid pumped into his body. Blood, now mixed with the toxic pink cocktail, ran through Steven's veins and out the orifices and gaping wounds in his body. The hum of the motor echoed in the room. The Angel Killer went limp as he was embalmed alive.

Freddy spat on the corpse. "Fucker!"

"A little help would be nice," George said, wincing.

Freddy ran to him to assess the damage, then retrieved the first-aid kit in the kitchen. He went to work bandaging up his friend for the second time.

"Am I gonna die?" George said as he leaned his head against the wall.

"Yeah, probably," Freddy mocked.

"Really?" His droopy eyes flared open in horror.

"No, you idiot, you're not going to die."

His eyes drooped back down in exhaustion, and he grinned. "So, is he dead now?"

Freddy looked back at the body on the table. Blood and pink liquid flowed down the table and gurgled into the drain. "Yeah, he's definitely dead."

"Good. Next time I'll have you check to see if they're dead." He pointed at him, "Don't ever fucking ask me again."

"Come on, you big baby, get up." Freddy helped him to his feet. George was shaky. Freddy said, "Stay there."

"Okay, boss."

He retrieved a candy bar from the drawer nearby. He quickly tore the top off and handed the Snickers(™) Bar to George.

"You eat food in here?" George asked in disgust.

"You know, well, you get hungry sometimes. Just eat it. You need your blood sugar to go up."

George took a bite. "Oh yeah, that's fucking good."

"Alright, you just rest a bit. I'm gonna start getting things cleaned up."

"Sounds good."

Freddy turned, surveyed the room. He took a deep breath, exhaled, and began the work. After a little while, George's energy returned, and he got up to help him.

Freddy texted his boss, Bob, to let him know that he would be leaving early. Bob responded with no problem and said he didn't have to work on Halloween anyway. This was all part of the plan to cover their tracks.

As George mopped all the floors, Freddy went to the security system and found the video coverage. He erased everything—the entire day. After triple checking the system for any trace of him and George, he walked around the offices to see if he could spot anything out of the ordinary. He couldn't do anything about the scratch marks on the walls from his glove, but that was part of the plan as well.

"So, do you think this is gonna work?" George asked.

"Yeah, everything is erased. Floors cleaned of all the blood. We left all of the damage in the kitchen, casket room, and walls. We will say it was a break-in. Probably teenage kids on Halloween. Just one more thing to do."

They stood in the crematory, staring at the oven.

"So, it's done?" George asked.

Freddy didn't respond. He opened it. Steven Murdock, The Angel Killer, was nothing but a pile of dust. They both stared at the pile.

George said, "We fucking did it, man. We actually killed this bad guy."

"Yeah, we did." He nodded and took a deep breath.

They continued to stare.

Freddy and George collected the remains and placed them into a plastic bag.

Freddy said, "Steven was supposed to be embalmed and buried in his gravesite. I changed the paperwork for cremation. He doesn't have anyone looking for him. They will bury his remains, and that's that."

George said, "This shit reminds me of your fucking movie."

"Why's that?" Freddy twisted the tie around the bag.

"I just hope we're not haunted by this motherfucker. Catch my drift?"

Freddy looked at him and grinned, "You scared?"

"Yeah, I'm fucking scared."

"Come on, Captain America, I'll save you. Speaking of that, we actually need to burn your clothes and mine. Blood residue and all. No traces."

"Oh yeah. Good idea."

Freddy began to take off his shirt.

"Now?" George asked.

"Yeah, dude, now. I'll throw them in the oven."

"Okay." George stripped.

Freddy flinched away. "Dude, where's your underwear?"

"You can't wear fucking undies with this costume, dude."

"What? Are you going to drive home like that?"

"No, I'm gonna wait for you to give me one of those fucking aprons and then drive home. With my ultimate fucking goal of not getting arrested."

Freddy got him an apron then retrieved the extra set of clothes he had in his office. They both left everything meticulously clean. The tools were wiped down, sterilized, and put away. Floors. Counters. Video coverage. Everything.

George retrieved a crowbar from his car. Freddy stared at his friend's lily-white ass as the apron only covered the front. George struggled to keep the flimsy material from blowing up while he walked. Freddy laughed to himself, bringing up his hand to cover his smirk.

They broke the back kitchen door open with a lot of muscle. The lock mechanism was broken while it was open to help the process along. They slumped to the ground in exhaustion, sweat dripping down their faces.

George said, "The ground is cold on my ass."

Freddy chuckled through labored breaths. "Let's just rest for a minute."

"It's hard to explain but, this was the worst and best fucking Halloween ever."

Freddy looked at George, "This has to be buried with us. No one can know. Not Jenny. Not your shrink. No one."

George looked at him, "For sure."

"C'mon, let's go."

They both got into their cars after removing the latex gloves. George saluted him, then took off. Freddy looked at his phone. He had one final thing to do. Erase the audio recording.

He hesitated at first. He wanted to play it back for some reason.

"No," he said aloud. "Just delete it."

The prompt was up.

Delete.

Yes or No.

CHAPTER 39
THE KISS OF REDEMPTION

It was December 11th, 2016. A blustery sixty-degree day on the coast of Encinitas. Wearing a black suit and a purple tie, George Casey stood at the front of the huge glass window sliders that opened up to his back patio.

He looked at his cell to get the time. It was 4:44 pm then slipped it back into his pocket and waited.

Freddy leaned over and said, "Right on time, my friend."

George didn't look at him. With lips barely moving, "I can't believe you talked me into this."

Mrs. Carrino entered the living room from the back of the house. She nodded to the boys and then walked over to them.

A minute later, Mr. Carrino escorted his daughter out of the hallway. She wore her original wedding dress from their marriage ceremony some seven years ago. There was no music, but Freddy heard it playing in his mind. Jenny radiated beauty. Always had and always will. It was the reason he had her wedding band engraved 'Always'.

Her smile lit up the room as Freddy made eye contact with her. Mr. and Mrs. C. also looked at each other, as the occasion ignited the memory of their own wedding day almost forty years prior.

George said, "Who gives this woman to be married to this man, again?"

"Her mother and I do...again." Mr. Carrino responded with a smile. He handed her hand over to Freddy and kissed his daughter's cheek. His eyes became glassy as he took in the magnitude of the moment. He turned to stand with his wife, who greeted him with a loving smile before they locked arms and watched on proudly.

"Dearly beloved," George began, "I've gathered you all here today—"

Freddy coughed on purpose. George got the hint.

"Right, just fucking with you. Oops, sorry, Mrs. C."

She half-smiled her forgiveness.

George refocused, "Hey guys, I just want to say what an honor it is to be here and to be officiating your wedding. I've never done this and probably never will again." Everyone chuckled and looked around at one another, believing his words to be true. He continued, "I thank the God you both now profess for bringing each of you into my life. You have shown me what true love is and that it is worth fighting for, no matter the pain and setbacks of life. And with that, let's proceed down my checklist," he said as he pulled out a crumpled piece of paper with notes and marks all over it. Jenny and Freddy giggled. Freddy whispered, "Unbelievable."

George looked up at him, "What, you want to do this? I'm nervous, dude." He went back to scanning his notes and mumbled, "Wait for bride, check. Smile as they walk, check. Handoff to Freddy, check. Intro, check. Aaaaannnnddddd, yes, now exchange vows." He looked up at them all staring at him. He stuffed the paper back into his pocket and smiled.

Freddy urged, "You ready?"

George scrunched his face, "Born ready, dude. Okay, now let's exchange some vows. Freddy, you're up to bat."

Freddy looked right into Jenny's eyes. He took a deep breath and exhaled, "Jenny, you have seen me at my worst. You have loved me at my lowest. But you haven't yet seen my best. My best will be to never leave your side again. To never abandon you. To always fight for you. To always believe in you. To always love you, no matter what this world throws at us. The evil of this world fought to keep us separated, but now I see the love of God is bigger and fought to keep us together." Freddy looked around at everyone and addressed them all, "I know this whole God thing is new to me, but I want you all to know that I have enough room in my heart for all of you. This marriage is about all of us."

George interjected, "Does that mean I get to sleep over at your place tonight?"

Mrs. C hissed, "George!"

"Oh, sorry, Mrs. C, it was a joke."

Freddy looked at George, "Thank you, my friend, for always being there for us. Jenny and I love you dearly. And we hope and pray that you were able to get everything on our wedding gift list we sent you." Everyone laughed.

"We shall see," he said.

Freddy turned his attention back to his bride, "Jenny, my sweet Jenny, thank you for saying yes. Thank you for being my partner for the rest of my life. My life is yours. I would die for you."

Jenny's eyes were sparkling. She smiled at him as his words washed over her heart. Unconsciously, she tilted her head and parted her lips as if to kiss him right then and there but caught herself.

"Jenny, please share your vows to Freddy," George said.

She refocused and took a deep breath. She exhaled, "Freddy, I love you. My love for you would walk through the fires of hell or the glaciers of heaven to be with you. You know the deep scars I carry. You know, and yet you still love me. You are the man I want to be with forever. You know the tears I've shed that no one else knows. You are the man I want to be with forever. You know the dreams I have. You are the man I want to fulfill those dreams with. It is this day that I say yes to be with you, but it is also a day that God has blessed us, and he is a redeeming God." Jenny slowly pulled something out of the hidden pocket in her dress—a pregnancy test.

Freddy instantly knew what it was and saw the positive indicator.

"I'm pregnant," she said through tears.

Freddy launched himself at Jenny and kissed her.

Mr. and Mrs. C beamed with joy, and they kissed.

George tried to get them to stop from entering into the sacred kiss marked for the end of the ceremony. It wasn't time yet. "Oh, well," he said, "Fuck it. You may kiss your bride. By the power given to me by the marriage ministry website and the state of California, I now pronounce you husband and wife." He paused. They continued to kiss and ignore him. "You see how it doesn't work very well? You guys kind of went out of order. No big deal. Everyone else fucking does it the right way, but no, you guys just wanted to go against the norm. I get it."

No one was listening to George. Mr. and Mrs. Carrino began to clap and cheer. George joined in the celebration and then whistled loudly. "Let's party!"

CHAPTER 40
THE DARK WALTZ

I T WAS ONE in the morning, New Year's day, 2017. George and Freddy sat in George's car outside the driveway, looking at the single-story home.

"I can't believe you bought us a house." He took another sip of his Dalmore single malt twenty-five-year-old scotch. His eyes in a daze as he stared ahead.

"Yeah, well, I didn't want my friends raising a family in some shithole apartment."

Freddy turned to look at him. He was a little inebriated, "Why do you do it? I mean, you just keep fucking giving us stuff and never want anything in return."

"You don't fucking get it, dude." He turned to look at him. "You're all I've got. I told myself a long time ago, George, you fucking find someone that cares and stick with them."

"So you think I care?"

"Well, to be honest, I thought it originally meant a chick until you came along."

Freddy raised his glass, "To people who care."

They clinked glasses and took a sip.

Freddy relaxed in the leather seat, stretching his legs out further, and rested his head back.

George said, "So why did you want to come out and sit in the car?"

"I didn't want anyone to overhear us."

"Overhear what? Our bad jokes."

"No, just your bad jokes. Mine are good."

"Oh yeah, fuck you." He chuckled.

They sat in silence for ten seconds.

George said, "Freddy?"

"Yeah."

"Are you seeing shit? I mean, like, things in shadows, and…"

Freddy turned toward him with a quizzical look. "What do you mean? Are you seeing ghosts?"

"I don't know. It's just creepy shit. I can't get what happened out of my head, dude. I think I sometimes see Steven in the shadows. It's like he's gonna jump out and get me or something. The whole thing is fucking with my mind," George confided.

"That's what I wanted to talk to you about."

"It's happening to you too?"

"Yes and no. It feels like it happened yesterday, and it also feels like it was decades ago."

"Same here. I wake up thinking it was a dream and then realize, no, that shit actually fucking happened. Then I get a little panicky." He paused and looked hard at Freddy, "Maybe we should talk to Dr. Beckman, dude."

"No fucking way!"

George held out his hands defensively, "Why not? It will be totally confidential. We don't have to use names or maybe just say it's a recurring nightmare. I don't know. Something."

"George, listen. We can't tell anyone about this. I mean it. Not even a nightmare theory. We can talk to each other and walk this out. Over time it will lessen. I promise."

"Really? Lessen?"

"Yeah, really. I've seen dead bodies my whole life, and it doesn't have any effect on me. It's just normal."

"Okay, so psychopath killers coming back from the dead to be killed with our hands will be normal? Check. Got it. It totally makes sense now. C'mon, are you listening to yourself?"

Freddy took a deep breath and sat back into his chair. "You're right. It's all fucked up. I just know that talking to the shrink will open up an entirely new problem for us."

"I don't know, dude. She goes deep, and I just feel like she's going to find out or something. It's like she reads my fucking mind."

"George, she's not reading your mind. She's reading your emotions, your reactions."

"Maybe."

"Maybe? C'mon. Maybe you should see someone else."

"No fucking way. Dana is hot and, I don't know, she gets me."

"She gets you? What does that mean?"

George stared at him.

Freddy said, "So, what, you see her because she is hot? You want to tap that or something?"

"Nooo, I don't want to 'tap that.' She just fucking gets me, is all. She helps me process my feelings and shit."

"Okay, I'm not your shrink, big guy, and certainly don't want to hear about your jerking off sessions after you see her."

"Whatever." George downed his drink.

They sat in silence once again. The smell of the new leather and liquor permeated their senses.

George said softly, "Is there a heaven?"

Freddy didn't respond. George turned his head to look at him and Freddy met his gaze.

"I don't know, but apparently, there's a hell. I can guess there's something out there."

"Well, aren't you a Christian now and shit?"

Freddy chuckled, "So that means I suddenly know about heaven?"

"Sure, why not?"

"I think I need to go to church or something to find out."

"Church? Really? You?"

"Why not me? Why not you?"

"Me, fuck that. I'd burn up as soon as I entered the parking lot."

"Why don't we go together?"

"Fuck you. You want to see me burned up?"

"No, dumb-ass. Not that. I mean, I'm interested in finding out more about heaven and hell stuff."

"Heaven and hell stuff?"

"Yeah. Heaven and hell stuff."

George looked long and hard at him. "If they start singing kumbaya shit then I'm out of there."

Freddy half-smiled, "I'll race you to the car if that happens."

George leaned back against the headrest. "Fuck me. Church. Can you believe it?"

Freddy leaned back also.

After a minute of them both contemplating actually entering a church, George shifted focus. He asked, "What about you, dude. How are you holding up?"

"Me? I don't know, to be honest." He sighed. "I just keep asking why Steven? Why did he come back from the dead and not the little girl?"

"I don't know, dude. I've asked the same. It's fucked up."

"Maybe it's not."

George sat up, "What do you mean?"

"I don't know. It's like I willed him back or something. Like I was destined to meet Steven, my inner demon face to face. For years I envisioned embalming him. To make him feel pain like no one else had. But in the end, I couldn't duplicate the pain of my own loss upon him."

"What are you getting at?"

Freddy turned to face him, "I don't feel closure. I still feel empty. The vengeance I had wasn't satisfied."

"But we got the motherfucker who killed Eve and all those others. What else were you looking for?"

"That's the thing. I don't know. I thought it was that, but it wasn't. I keep reliving that night over and over. I can still taste the sulfur in my mouth and smell the rotten stench in my nose." Freddy drifted into the memory; the event replayed in his mind. "I can hear him whispering in my ear that night and all the things he told me. I can smell his breath, the lingering scent of the liquor, and stagnant air inside a corpse who had been dead for days." George's face scrunched up at the description. Freddy continued, "It was like he was still possessed. There was a presence or something. As he spoke to me, I heard distant whispers. They were gliding upon the words that came from his mouth."

"What, what, kind of whispers?" George asked shakily.

Freddy swallowed, looked at George, "Demonic whispers."

Suddenly, someone knocked on the window next to George. George screamed and jolted away.

"Hey," the voice muffled from the window between them, "what are you guys up to?"

"Holy shit, Mrs. C!" It was Jenny's mom. George clutched his shirt, trying to massage his heart through his chest. He looked over at Freddy. Both of them let out a deep breath.

George said, "Yeah, yeah, we're coming back in."

"Okay. We are getting ready to leave and wanted to say goodbye." She didn't wait for a response as she headed back inside, leaving them alone once again.

"Fuck me. I think I shit my pants," George said as he sat back. "Okay, I've got to get some sleep."

"Yeah, me too."

George opened his door and slid out. He noticed Freddy didn't move. "You coming?"

"What? Uh, yeah. I'll be there in a second."

George closed his door and headed back inside.

Freddy watched his best friend enter and close the front door behind him. His eyes meandered down to his phone. He entered his private code and then launched his recording app. There was only one recording. Pressing play, the scratches of the mic rubbing on his clothes echoed. Freddy's voice said, "It's alright. Just me. Just Freddy." Another jostle and scratching sound before he said, "So, why did they, uh, the demons, come for you?"

"To punish me."

"To punish you? Why?"

"I was wrong. I...I..."

"Wrong about what?"

Steven said, "You don't get it? They were right."

"Who was right?"

"He told us. We didn't listen."

Steven's voice was a matter of fact, "I am the way, the truth, the life. He was right."

"So, Steven, let's talk about the demons you mentioned. They came for you. Where did they take you?"

"Hell."

"Tell me what happened when you died."

Steven drifted back into his memory, "I lifted up into the air. I remember it being so beautiful. I could see...everyone. I saw myself on the grass. I couldn't hear anything at first. It was silent, peaceful." He swallowed hard. "Then I heard something. It was like a knife sliding against a metal pole. Screeching. I thought my eyes were seeing people drifting toward me. I was mesmerized by them. White angels, but no wings. Just white wispy looking cloth hiding faces beneath."

"What happened?"

"Demons! Their faces…They came for me. Slithery whispering voices of hate and violence. They wanted to shred my soul. They took me away…far away."

"To hell?" Freddy said.

"To hell!" His tone relaxed, "I can't go back…I can't."

"This is so crazy to me, Steven. So you are a hero, and yet they take you to hell? I don't get it."

"They'll take you too." There was a pause, "Unless…"

Freddy caught the sight of Jenny coming out from the front of the house. He quickly shut the recorded message of that night off. The message he didn't delete. The message he couldn't delete.

Jenny opened the driver's door. "You okay?"

He smiled, "Yeah, I'm good. Real good. Just thinking."

"About?"

"Us, our baby, our home."

She smiled. "Everyone's getting ready to leave. Come inside and say goodbye."

Freddy opened his door and exited. Jenny closed her door, and they came together, clasping hands and arms together as they entered their new home. Freddy had his wife back. He had a child on the way. Deep down inside the recesses of his heart and mind, however, he wrestled with another reality. A reality outside of the one he had with Jenny. A reality of a different world that was reflected in the undeleted recording of October 31st, 2016. The night he went from believing there was nothing beyond this life to witnessing the miraculous raising of Steven Murdock back from the dead. This wasn't the first time he had played that recording. No, he had played it every day since. He listened to every breath, every nuance. He replayed it inside his head every day. He heard the whispers coming from someone besides Steven or himself. It was supernatural. It was there, and he needed to find out for himself what it was. Everything he once believed had been shattered that night.

Someone at a church must know the answers he needed. George was the only one who knew what happened, and Freddy needed his friend more than at any other time before. He couldn't do this alone.

But there was one secret Freddy kept to himself. Two secrets, to be exact. One, the recording of the event on his phone. Two, he hadn't stopped trying to raise more people from the dead.

EVERYONE HAD LEFT. Jenny was in the bathroom, brushing her teeth. Freddy sat on the edge of their bed when a text message came through. It was from Alice Cooper.

HAPPY NEW YEAR. IM GONNA BE IN TOWN NEXT WEEK. LETS CONNECT. I WANT TO HEAR WHAT YOU THOUGHT ABOUT THAT COCKROACH VIDEO. CRAZY RIGHT???

Freddy switched his phone off and looked up to see himself reflected in the mirror. His shirt was off, revealing the tattoos covering his chest and arms, and wrapping around to his back. As he stared, two images appeared on either side of him. Steven Murdock and his daughter Eve. Images he had seen often over these last two months. He had grown used to them now. They never spoke. They just watched him. Steven had a smug look while Eve grinned, her eyes beaming with joy. Always together. His mind allowed it, cherished it. Why? Because he could see his daughter so clearly. Clearer than any time before. Were they ghosts? He didn't know. But he did want to find out if they were real. What was on the other side of life? He had to know more. He was awakened, and now he needed to have answers.

He whispered, "Dad, you were wrong. There *is* something after death."

Jenny's head popped around the corner, toothbrush in her hand, white foamy toothpaste around her mouth, "Did you say something?"

He grinned at her, love in his eyes, and shook his head no. She smiled and went back to brushing. He heard the sink water come on. The sound drowned out his low voice.

Freddy refocused on the images staring back at him and said in a soft whisper, "1-2, Freddy's coming for you."

THE EMBALMER 2-
COMING SOON.

Go to the website and become an Embalmer follower.
Get all the latest and greatest information.

www.BraeWyckoff.com

ACKNOWLEDGMENTS

A big shout out to the fictional character, George Casey. He was a hit. Everyone who has read this book points out George being the true hero. Why? It was his tenacity for being a true friend to Freddy. He literally would do anything for Freddy. Thank you, George, for coming into my life. I look forward to future books with you. You are such the 'fucking giver'.

> *Proverbs 18:24 "One who has unreliable friends soon comes to ruin, but there is a friend who sticks closer than a brother."*

Thank you to my amazing beta readers, Claudene, Jill, CJ, Bre, Kyme, Fritzi, Rhonda, Rob, Rikah, Charlie, Kellye, Gloria, Charles, and Ben. All of your input made the story even better.

Thank you, Tiffany Vakilian, for your incredible editing prowess. Keep calling out BS on the areas of my writing that needs a good kick in the ass. You are a gem.

Thank you to all my fans. I really appreciate you going on these incredible journeys with me.

I saved the best for last. Thank you to my amazing wife, Jill Elizabeth Wyckoff. Without your support and encouragement, it would be unknown where I would be today. I love you always.

OTHER BOOKS BY BRAE WYCKOFF

Young Adult Epic Fantasy Series: (won multiple awards)

The Orb of Truth
The Dragon God
The Vampire King

Historical Fiction:
(won 5-Star Readers Favorite Award and has movie rights pending)

Demons & Thieves

FUN FACTS WITHIN
THE EMBALMER:

The cockroach video was true. The video has been taken down for several years now, but I posted it originally on July 22nd, 2012, on The Greater News website where we report on miracles all around the world. I watched in amazement of the two gentlemen calling a cockroach back to life and it happened.

www.TheGreaterNews.com

http://www.thegreaternews.com/blog/2/26/2013/
bug-supernaturally-raised-from-the-dead

Hollywood Vampires is Alice Cooper's tribute band. The date it happened is the exact date in the book.

Tuesday, May 24, 2016, at Turning Stone in New York

Hollywood Vampires played from 8:13 to 9:52 p.m., with plenty of classic rock covers and several original songs co-written by Depp.

Raise the Dead (original)

I Got a Line on You (Spirit)

20th Century Boy (T. Rex)

Pinball Wizard (The Who)

My Generation (The Who)

Manic Depression (Jimi Hendrix)

Cold Turkey (John Lennon)

Come Together (The Beatles)

7 and 7 Is (Arthur Lee, Love)

Whole Lotta Love (Led Zeppelin)

Five to One/Break on Through (The Doors)

Rebel Rebel (David Bowie)

Suffragette City (David Bowie)

As Bad As I Am (original)

Stop Messin' Around (Aerosmith)

Dead Drunk Friends (original)

Ace of Spades (MotAPrhead)

I'm Eighteen (Alice Cooper)

Sweet Emotion (Aerosmith)

Encore

Train Kept a Rollin' (Aerosmith)

School's Out (Alice Cooper)

CINESPIA October 22, 2016: A Nightmare on Elm Street

This was a real event (Robert Englund was not there, however).

Location: Hollywood Forever Cemetery in Los Angeles

San Diego, CA- I used actual street names and locations. (The mortuary where Freddy works is fictitious)

Lastly, *Wasting June is an actual band.* It is my son's band, Thomas Modifica Jr. Used with his permission. You can hear the songs on YouTube. Wasting June: Mortadella. You can purchase the songs on Amazon and iTunes.

https://www.youtube.com/channel/
UCtmFcdhQHKRUOfj0B2CPxIQ

ABOUT THE AUTHOR

Brae Wyckoff is an award-winning and internationally acclaimed author, born and raised in San Diego, CA. He has been married to his beautiful wife, Jill, since 1993, and they have three children and seven wonderful grandchildren. He loves story-telling, his family and friends, and living the fullest life possible that brings meaning and purpose to himself and others.

Brae is an open book and welcomes everyone to contact him. If you would like to have Brae Wyckoff come out and speak at any event, book club, author signing, please email him directly.

braewyckoff@gmail.com

You can find Brae on all the social media channels.

CPSIA information can be obtained
at www.ICGtesting.com
Printed in the USA
BVHW081141310721
613282BV00004B/93